HOMESTEAD SECRETS

Noelene Jenkinson

Chapter 1

'I'm being sidelined?' Addie Kendall couldn't believe what she was hearing.

She narrowed her gaze, analysing Morgan Ross, the company CEO seated opposite across his impressive cedar desk, his face a mask of steel control. Her departmental boss, Steve Wilson stood to one side, legs crossed, leaning against bookshelves. Throughout the meeting the men had exchanged loaded glances.

Ten minutes earlier she had optimistically assumed her revelation would be met with horror and a request to jump right onto the embarrassing and potentially criminal predicament that could ruin the Company's reputation and endanger the security of a rival. If it leaked. She had not expected this condescending evasive attitude and air of casual disinterest, leaving her speechless and suspicious. As though Addie was the one at fault. Damn it. She had *found* the problem.

'No, not at all,' Morgan hastily replied, 'but your findings warrant top level discretion and investigation to identify the alleged breach.'

Alleged? She had seen the evidence for herself. Someone in this building had hacked into another competitor company's system with the potential to steal their data and information. If they hadn't already. Addie took a deep breath, ignoring the insult and stunned by the management brush off.

'As head of our departmental team,' she emphasised, glaring at Steve, still waiting for his support, 'I'm best placed and the most logical choice to find and expose the culprit. I found the violation.' Why wasn't he backing her up?

'I take your point,' Morgan Ross said easily, 'but to avoid any confusion or,' he hesitated, '*misunderstanding* as to where the problem originated, we believe it's best if you take a temporary leave of absence while we handle it. We'll call you.' Another pause. 'If we need you again.'

Astounded, Addie took in the implications of their recommendation. This was no suggestion. It was an order. A definite company demand. Right from the top. And she hadn't missed the inference to *if* they needed her again, not *when*.

She didn't believe this. The bastards. 'You need to warn the other company.'

That urgency alone held challenging implications for Addie. On the one hand, presumed loyalty to her employer company. On the other, a bond with their opposition and the family company at risk going back to childhood. Demanding her personal integrity above all other considerations.

Morgan Ross rose, signifying the end of the

discussion. 'We'll deal with it from here. Thank you for raising your concerns.'

She was being dismissed? Right now from where she sat, neither suit in this office looked like they had any immediate intention of doing anything. At least not in any hurry. They didn't give a shit! Why not? She would have asked Steve but she was already looking at his back as he crossed the room and opened the door.

'We'll keep in touch, Addie,' Morgan Ross said, already seated again, head down and shuffling papers.

Addie and Steve travelled down together in the lift to their IT level in silence. Clamping down on her contempt, she resisted asking how much he was being paid to keep quiet. He was known for keeping his eye on the top rung of the Carlton Ross ladder and taking any opportunity to slide into the boss' favour. Scowling, she wondered exactly what this company was hiding. And why? Whatever the cover-up, Steve was implicated up to his neck.

When the elevator doors slid open, Addie ignored her boss, strode toward her area, shut down her computer station, grabbed her shoulder bag and denim jacket to head out.

'Where are you off to?' James asked, eyebrows raised, her closest friend and most trusted ally in this workplace.

'Just leaving early for the weekend.' Good thing it was Friday and she could use the excuse.

'Farm?'

She nodded, managed a weak smile and brief wave and bolted. They would find out on Monday morning that she wasn't coming back, apparently not any time soon. Addie hadn't left in a rush because she was humiliated or afraid but because the matter was urgent and timing vital.

Riding the lift down to street level, Addie fumed. The Carlton Ross company might not take this breach seriously and with any sense of purpose in favour of their opposition competitor, but she did. Already her active brain was churning over how she could achieve that on her parents' Wimmera farm 300 kilometres from her office computer without company access.

Whoever followed up her discovery needed to investigate *now*. Every second counted. As soon as Addie revealed the problem, Morgan Ross himself should have been on the phone to Chandler Digital, the exposed company. Warn their opposition not only about the potential security leak and threat it imposed but alert them to the obvious weakness in their system. Everyone knew how vulnerable that left them to exploitation of sensitive information. All too embarrassing for Ross but Addie was convinced that alone was not the reason for the cover up.

Her mind was distracted as the lift doors slid open and she joined the crush of fellow workers leaving the building early. While it was their chance to voluntarily escape for the weekend and she would never refuse a visit home to the Wimmera, she herself had been firmly pushed.

The mild early autumn breeze whipped down Collins Street between skyscraper towers, car horns echoed, trams clanged their way ferrying people to other connections or suburbs.

God, she hated the city but this was where her career prospects lay. There wasn't much call in small rural towns for an IT security specialist. Addie had been lured by a generous six figure salary allowing her the luxury of a scarily high but affordable inner city rental.

With virtually no social life and making use of cheap public transport, it kept her savings plan alive to achieve her dream. Setting up and remotely running her own IT security business from some, as yet, unknown location in the country far away from urban noise and exposure. But first she needed to establish her name and reputation, while making valuable industry connections.

All of which was now in jeopardy. All those hours of work and years of loyalty. For nothing. Heading back to square one loomed large and seemed a definite possibility.

But the significant job had enabled her to buy the desirable classic EH Holden back home from their elderly neighbour, Bill Schafer. Fondly named Gertie, it had sat in tantalising safety under canvas in one of his sheds for decades. Her brother Nick restored the classic vehicle and reconditioned the motor until it hummed.

Addie parked it in her barely adequate shoebox of a garage space that went with her Fitzroy terrace rental. The old gem only saw the light of day every other weekend when she returned to the farm. Her escape and breathing space from the loneliness and isolation of family, back to her roots and reality.

Her employer company, Carlton Ross, had chosen the east end of the city in a more traditional location and style, renovating a three storey heritage building.

Other newer and more upmarket concerns chose the open space of renovated warehouses with vaulted ceilings and original brickwork, introducing skylights, quiet work areas, meeting spaces, cafes and courtyards.

Like Chandler Digital.

Addie sighed, thinking of Harry, knowing what she had to do.

As she waited at her tram stop and eventually boarded her usual number 11 on Collins Street heading for her digs, her thoughts pushed the reality of a busy city and her fellow commuters aside, returning to the cause of her temporary release from work.

Who in Carlton Ross would do that? To a limited extent, Addie understood their reluctance to investigate one of their own supposedly trustworthy staff. It reflected badly on the company and looked damned fishy. The fact that the corruption came from their building would be a hard pill for management to swallow but surely business ethics dictated the offender be identified and fired, and their opposition company informed of the breach.

And of course the next question that immediately sprang to mind was *why*? What reasoning lay behind such an illegal dishonest action? And then there was the risk of being discovered and unmasked, which was Addie's job as a trusted top IT professional in the organisation.

Was the person being pressured by someone? Was it done for kicks just to prove it could? It had to be someone with the expertise to break and infiltrate another company's system. That narrowed the field to someone like Addy or a handful of her fellow workmates.

Strange that she had been asked to step aside because her team was highly skilled to nose out the culprit. She had found the leak and reported it but needed more time to identify the offender. Which meant she must start by searching out the dirt on every possible suspect and their financial situation.

Computer crimes were usually all about greed. If anyone acquired secret research and product development information, it could be worth millions. Who needed money badly enough to risk everything, and why?

She had brought the anomaly on the Carlton

Ross company computer system to their attention yet had been fobbed off. Something stank. The word *scapegoat* came to mind but she intended to cover her backside against that eventuality and already had an appointment in place.

Growing up in the country, Addie had continued as she started out. By never conforming and ignoring expectations. At job interviews, that meant no female power suits. She was far more comfortable in casual trousers or jeans, tee shirts, a denim jacket and boots. Clothes didn't affect her work outcomes. A whizz with figures and computers, she was paid to get results and delivered.

Why then would her employer remove her from the very kind of task for which she was qualified?

Bernie Grant, head of Human Resources at Carlton Ross, eyed his company CEO, Morgan Ross, and the antique mechanical clock behind him on the wall with equal amounts of annoyance and frustration.

Firstly, not only was that damn thing noisy, ticking away 24/7 but the cleaners had to wind it. Frankly, Bernie didn't see the point although he got that, in this digital age, it was a nod to old technology.

And secondly, doing what Morgan asked would make him late home tonight and disrupt his weekend. Again.

But you never challenged a Ross, least of all this one. His job was on the line here. It was either comply and work overtime or scan the Situations Vacant in the weekend newspapers.

Like Addie Kendall. He would take on a bet from anyone she would never be welcomed back into the company fold. Being the smartest nerd in IT, she had probably already worked that one out.

Whereas he was switched on to people and their mindset. Could read and manipulate them at will. Shuffle personnel as deftly as a pack of cards. Was an expert of *redistribution*. The boss knew it, he knew it, so yet again he had been called in to complete an assignment no matter how it intruded on his personal life.

Not that the boss cared if he even had one. As always, Liz would go ballistic when he checked in late. But she was aware of his annual bonus and he knew how to handle her. His focus would continue to be making himself irreplaceable.

'Keep up the pressure on Kendall. Texts, emails, the lot,' Morgan barked.

'Yes, Sir.'

'Don't let up.'

Bernie shook his head. 'How long?'

'The usual. Until we resolve this mess and can safely let her go.'

Ongoing then. Wow, this must be some serious shit. His best opportunity yet to perform on this one. Showcase his skills.

'If that doesn't work we'll try a more

personal approach,' Morgan blathered on. 'We need to keep pushing. It's our company and my personal reputation on the line here this time, Grant.'

'Of course, Sir.'

'Make it happen.'

'Consider it done.'

Morgan stood, moved around the vast desk and slapped his employee on the shoulder. 'Good man.'

Once out of the office, Bernie mentally rubbed his hands together even as he heard the door slam behind him. If he pulled off this one, his job was secure and he might even suggest a substantial raise. A hint, like blackmail. A gentle nudge to his advantage.

It wasn't until she had stepped off the tram and strode for her terrace, that Addie checked her phone. An email from the company already? Someone was under orders to work fast. Probably Bernie since he led HR and if this was a cover-up, it had to be a yes man. No lackey would suffice. The powers at the top would need to keep their secret up there.

She considered ignoring it but the banner preview on her phone caught her interest so, wisely or not, she opened her mail to cynically scan the letter. Her swift gaze skipped words to read the gist. Something about "*…being reassured this leave of absence is only temporary…*" and "*…a* *rigorous and independent investigation will be carried out."*

Two lies right there. Shaking her head, Addie closed her phone. After she sorted out this situation, intuition told her she would be seeking another contract.

So, first things first. She had discovered the violation only hours ago. This being a weekend meant less chance of sharp-eyed detection until Monday. Fingers crossed. Because she had to set wheels in motion from her end. Fast.

All her suspicions pointed to Morgan Ross protecting himself. For whatever reason. Which she intended to find out. And worse, at the expense of a highly successful and now vulnerable competitor, Chandler Digital.

Disturbing because the Chandler and Kendall kids grew up in the Wimmera and went to school together. Until university. And her own personal rift.

These days, rarely in touch any more, the two families privately followed each other's family doings and successes from a distance. While Addie's parents remained on their wheat farm, the Chandler parents and Harry had moved to Melbourne leaving their younger son, Oliver, to manage their Merino sheep stud property.

So Addie's difficult obligation was to make the call. Not on her mobile. Long before the latest cold email, distrust had set in. There was a public phone near her terrace. She would use that.

Addie walked like a robot to her row cottage and dumped her gear in the tiny hall. First, she sat on her bed and phoned home on her mobile. No danger there and totally not necessary to warn the folks of her imminent arrival. Having raised and fed three sons and a tomboy daughter alongside their father, Darren, her mum Julie was always well provisioned. Accustomed to the comings and goings of her adult tribe. Besides, right at this moment, Addie needed to hear her mother's warm-hearted voice.

'You came home last weekend.' A note of concern crept into her mother's voice. 'Everything all right?'

'Yep. Have a chance to work off site for a while.'

'ETA?'

'Late-ish. Eight or nine. I can grab something at the Coach.'

'Nonsense. I'll keep your dinner warm.'

'Thanks Mum. I'll text when I'm close.'

'Take care, darling. Oh, and Adrianna?'

She grinned to herself. 'Mm?'

'Be lovely having you home longer.'

'Don't be soppy. I'll be a nuisance.'

'Never. Love you.'

'Love you back.'

Addie hung up, boosted by the brief conversation, and then sauntered along to the payphone box. *This* call wouldn't be so easy.

She needed to offer a confession and in the

same breath, ask for help. Just the thought of it felt like walking through an ants nest straight into danger. She was already up to her neck in something she didn't yet understand so how hard could it be facing her teenage torment after all this time?

Addie had never been able to either tolerate or forgive betrayal. Making this phone call meant breaking their five year silence which she vowed she would never do, expecting him to make the first move. Hadn't happened yet.

She toyed with the handset before drawing a deep breath, dropping in her coins and pressing the company number. After being transferred, she jumped when he answered, expecting to go through a PA or be told he was busy and only able to leave a message.

'Harrison Chandler.' As always, the voice was deep and soothing.

So official. 'Hi Harry,' she said brightly. 'It's…um…Addie-'

'Kid?' There was a pause.

To her embarrassment, he used her childhood nickname, short for echidna because of its long snout and sensors. Addie was notorious for always being nosy, interrupting conversations, asking questions. Back then, she hadn't minded being teased and labelled so much. Now, it just plain annoyed. Not the best start to the conversation. On the flipside, he didn't sound displeased by the contact.

'Yes. This is a business call.' Just so he knew. 'I need to see you urgently. Can we meet?'

A heartbeat's pause, could have been shock, then, 'Of course.'

'It's important to your family's company.'

'Really?' Another hesitation while he processed her request. 'You can't tell me over the phone?'

At least she had him interested and cooperative. 'No. Too risky. Somewhere private, like, soon.'

'Where are you?'

'I'm heading home for the weekend but-'

'As it happens I have a family event this weekend on the farm.' He paused, sounding pressed. 'I should already be on the highway. Oliver's engaged.'

Preoccupied with her job fiasco, she hadn't heard the news. How ignorant was that! Addie felt mildly ashamed of temporarily forgetting her country roots and district neighbours.

'That's great news. I'll tell the folks.'

'It's already been in the local rag.'

'Oh.' Her mother hadn't mentioned it. 'Well, can you spare some time?'

'Big family dinner tonight but I could probably steal an hour late tomorrow before the official function.'

Damn, almost twenty four hours away. Time was ticking. But she would rather meet on home turf than here in the city. It was less a matter of discomfort than a need for distance from the problem. 'Okay. How about the hollow down by the creek. It's sheltered and private. We won't be seen.'

'No we certainly won't.' He sounded amused.

Surely he didn't think- 'I'll be camping,' she pointed out. That way her folks and equally nosy brothers wouldn't be around either. 'And don't come through the farm. Use the back way. Off the main road down the lane to the paddock. I'll leave the gate open. You know the way.'

'Sounding more mysterious by the minute.'

'Just a precaution. Do as I ask, Harry, please.' A note of urgent appeal crept into her voice. 'It's important.'

'Sounds mysterious but sure. Of course.'

He sounded irritable but he had never liked being told what to do. Which made them too similar and incompatible. Addie sighed, grateful that at least he had agreed to meet. Her professional reputation and career were at stake, and his family's company future depended on it.

Addie's hands shook as she hung up. She reminded herself it was not about competition this time, it was about ethics. Back in her terrace, she packed a big bag and stowed it in her old Holden boot.

Paranoid about being watched or trailed – would Carlton Ross stoop that low? – she strode from her side street and row of old workers' cottages onto Brunswick Street, having already plotted the route she needed to take.

Glancing around casually from time to time and stopping to look in shop windows to see what was happening behind her, she strolled as though browsing with all the time in the world, trusting any stalkers might be fooled. Meanwhile her thoughts functioned at light speed brainstorming ideas to confront the dreaded meeting with Harry tomorrow knowing that, ideally, it should be way sooner.

Addie entered a café and walked straight through to its rear entrance off the service lane that ran behind the length of shops to a law office a few doors down. An unnecessary action maybe but dealing with Carlton Ross, a body soon learned to take every precaution.

She had met her workmate, James' friend and very sharp lawyer, Jade, at the local pub one Friday night soon after starting with Carlton Ross. James' attempt to widen her local social circle. At this early stage of her employment drama, the appointment was just covering her backside in case the company slapped her with anything remotely legal. More likely than not, she predicted.

Almost immediately, Jade ushered her into the humble office where Addie poured out every possible detail of how this afternoon's events had played out. She had also copied the incriminating computer evidence onto a USB and left that as security with Jade for safe keeping. Ironically, Addie had taken the little piece of technology into her meeting with Morgan Ross and Steve Wilson ready to hand it over but after sizing up the atmosphere in the office and being rushed from the building, kept it firmly in her pocket. So far, it was the only scrap of evidence she had but she needed to delve deeper.

Once the paperwork and formalities in the legal office were done, the two women chatted until Jade's law clerk announced her next appointment and Addie left.

Now she could begin the fight back.

One foot in front of the other and one day at a time may prove damn tiresome. She just wanted this mess sorted but Morgan Ross wasn't known for his honesty or retreat in a contest. Two things she had discovered to her disadvantage today.

Fresh out of university and loaded with glowing degrees attesting to her ability, Addie only had eyes for a big company contract and the salary that went with it. So she had breezed right into the Carlton Ross fold, too trusting and now learned her mistake. The hierarchy was toxic. On reflection, hints of preferential promotions in her Section came to mind. For all of which, to her growing frustration, she had been overlooked.

Then today, too clever for her own good, she had stumbled on suspicious company irregularities and was on the brink of uncovering the culprit when she was summoned to see the boss himself.

Alert to the reason for a call to the top executive floor, Addie was ushered into the boss' sanctum as his PA quietly shut the door. Despite her protests and explanations, because her computer history showed searches in the area of contention, accusations came thick and fast.

Somehow Addie had survived the horrific interrogation with deep breaths and composed replies. Denial was pointless. Ross needed a scapegoat and Addie won the label.

She didn't know which was worse. The smug announcement from Ross, eyes narrowed, sneer on his lips, or the frustrating walk out through the general office cubicles on the way to the lifts and her *leave of absence*.

Whatever the reason behind this ambush, she needed to warn the Chandlers, sort out the baloney and clear her name.

Chapter 2

Addie had barely cleared city traffic heading west on the freeway for Ballarat and the Wimmera beyond, when her mobile rang. She flicked a glance. Bernie Grant. Interesting. Against her better judgement and annoyed to have her steady highway run interrupted, she pulled over and answered on speaker.

'Is this to tell me you've found the culprit?' Cheeky but she couldn't resist.

She didn't imagine the uncomfortable pause. Based on her usual composure at work, Bernie would never have anticipated her blast. But then she hadn't been victimised by Carlton Ross before either.

'Addie,' he said wryly. 'Did you get our email?'

'Yes. All of them. You can stop harassing me. Unless you already have evidence proving my innocence.' If she didn't keep her sense of humour, she would go nuts.

'You know we couldn't possibly in such a short time,' Bernie muttered.

'Of course you couldn't. Not without me.' The gloves were off the moment she had walked out of the Carlton Ross offices ninety minutes ago. 'Someone set me up and you know it. Trace the true source from the system and you'll find your man.'

'Or woman.'

'In Carlton Ross? The only one in IT is on a *leave of absence*.' When first employed, Addie had thought she was blazing a trail for other women to follow. 'Kind of narrows the field, doesn't it? If you find another reason to bother me, do it through my lawyer. I'll text you her details. She's expecting contact.'

Addie turned off her phone then resumed her trip. By the time the soft humps of the blue grey Grampians mountains came and went on her left, emerging onto the bleached stubble paddocks of open plains Wimmera country, Addie was stiff and desperate for a stretch. So when the familiar landmark Coach Roadhouse appeared ahead, she pulled in.

Built on the site of an original Cobb and Co coaching inn and horse changing station, the privately owned district icon provided quality home style cooking and warm hospitality, compliments of its quirky owners, brother and sister, Sid and Gracie Townsend and their loyal local staff.

Today, Gracie and her friendly long term employee Holly Duncan were behind the counter.

'Hey Addie,' Holly greeted. 'Home to the farm for the weekend?'

'Bit longer. Taking a short break.'

'Might see you around then. What can we get you?'

Addie set her keep mug on the counter. 'Fill that up with my usual black tea and maybe one of Sid's pastries.' She eyed off the sweet baking display cabinet and sighed. 'And fill a box for Mum. You choose.'

Holly grinned. 'Sure.'

Although not a native of the Wimmera, outwardly at least the waitress always seemed so happy but, if Addie remembered correctly, about five years ago Holly's mother had gone missing in the district. Travelling from Melbourne, her last known movements had been in this region.

For whatever reason, Holly had moved here, perhaps to be closer to the last place her mother was sighted. So sad for her, not knowing what happened. Who knew if the truth would ever come to light?

Addie couldn't even begin to imagine what life must be like for the young woman carrying such a burden.

Fifteen minutes later, Addie was sipping her tea and turning off the highway just east of her home town, Horsham, heading for the family farm, dust billowing out behind her. With daylight saving still in play and not yet sunset, even at the steady pace of her old EH, Addie had made good time.

She turned in at the open gate and around to

the huge open-fronted vehicle sheds on the other side of the house. Both family dogs raced to greet her before her car had stopped. As she pulled in beside two utes, a four wheel drive, her Mum's silver sedan and a ride on mower, Rowdy the red heeler and kelpie Bandit barked and jumped all over her when she slid from the vehicle.

'Hey boys.'

They danced around her as she walked to the house, through the gate, along the short path surrounded by lawn and edged with her mother's hardy country garden then onto the broad undercover paved patio. Since no dogs were allowed indoors, the pair sat on their haunches, pink tongues hanging out, ears pricked, sharp eyes alert.

The screen door squeaked as Addie yanked it open and kicked off her boots to join the other farm footwear along one wall of the porch.

'In here,' her mother called out.

Where else would she be but in their huge farmhouse kitchen, the heart of their home, with its scrubbed timber table in the centre and kettle always on the boil?

Apron on and back to Addie as she worked at the big cream range with multiple ovens everyone called *the beast*, Julie Kendall half turned her cheek for the usual kiss. 'Good trip?'

Her daughter sidled up, drawn by the familiar aromas of a corned beef dinner, and supplied the expected greeting.

'What do you have there?' Julie eyed Addie's cardboard box.

'Treats from Sid at the Roadhouse.'

Her mother chuckled. 'They'll disappear fast around here.'

'They're for you, not hungry men. Hide them. I'll just dump my bag and be back to help.'

'No need. Almost done. Lachie's over at Jenny Campbell's for tea. Nick's still on duty at the garage in town and Mitch is with your father in the office doing phone deals selling grain.'

Addie hovered halfway to the passage door. 'How long has Lachie been seeing Jenny?'

'She made herself useful during harvest and they've been a *thing* ever since.'

Addie waggled her eyebrows. 'Interesting.' The blonde and suntanned Kendall brothers were notorious for being among the most handsome and eligible in the district. 'You might marry one of us off yet,' she quipped.

Her mother looked surprised. 'You met someone?'

Addie pulled a face. 'Not. And it certainly wouldn't be a city boy.'

She cringed with guilt as she headed for her bedroom, her mind distracted with thoughts of the urban cowboy she had arranged to meet tomorrow.

Before she returned to the kitchen, Addie stopped by the office, rewarded by her father's big smile and crushing hug, and a friendly punch on the arm from Mitch. He and Lachie seemed likely to take over the property in partnership if their father ever pulled back from farming.

Hard to imagine but Addie could see her parents retiring into town although she figured her Dad's ute would still find its way out to the farm every day.

To that end, for years now, he had been buying up small pieces of nearby land and the occasional lone paddock whenever they came on the market. One acquisition had a farmhouse on the property which was being maintained for either Lachie or Mitch to live. All with the aim of putting their farming succession in place.

Nick had already bought into the local garage and trucking business in town that came with a house next door. Although Addie loved country life, she knew and accepted she would always be welcome in the family home after her two farming brothers married. She and Nick would maintain a financial interest until Lachie and Mitch bought them out.

Over recent years, the Kendalls held an annual meeting so everyone knew what was happening now and in the future, all encouraged to voice their opinions.

Over dinner later, Addie tried forgetting her troubles amid the rowdy comfort of her family around the old kitchen table. Halfway through the meal, her mechanical genius brother, Nick, appeared, his skills always in demand in a farming community.

'Hey Sis.' He gave her a thumbs up, grabbed his plate of food from the warming oven and hoed in.

For a time Addie managed to shove her problems out of mind but, sitting out on the patio later star gazing in the mild evening, although she dearly loved every member of her family, knew she needed solitude at the moment to think.

Next morning, seeing her hauling camp gear and camera bags into the back of their old unregistered ute only used on the farm, and stocking the Engel cooler with food, Julie Kendall guessed her daughter's intentions.

'Be nice down by the creek.'

'Just for the weekend. Mitch catching any yabbies down there?' Her mother nodded. Addie made a mental note to throw in some fishing bait and her nets.

'Don't forget the two way.'

Addie rolled her eyes. Didn't matter how old you were, mothers were always mothers. 'As if.'

'I've made a double batch of scones. Take a handful.'

Addie had risen at sunup and taken the motorbike for a spin before breakfast to blow away the city cobwebs. She smelt her mother's baking as soon as she returned and entered the house. Her mother had a pile of blue first prize ribbons and certificates won at the annual agricultural show over many years.

'Can you let the guys know I don't want company?' The last thing Addie needed was anyone around when Harry showed up later. Julie raised her eyebrows but stayed silent. 'Work stuff, you know.'

Addie shrugged aside her mother's unspoken concern. Not a complete lie. Already she hated the deception yet had barely begun the quest of investigation and building her case.

Driving away from the farmhouse was bittersweet because now her troubles resurfaced and would become her sole focus with plans to set in motion. She already had a truck load of ideas. It was just a matter of working through each and putting those in place most likely to pull in evidence or yield definite results.

Of course, just to complicate matters, Harry was in the middle of it all. It would be a challenge not only seeing him again after so long but potentially working together. Cooperation was inevitable if she was to succeed but not knowing his reaction to her news, she had no idea what might eventuate.

Addie left the reserve paddock gate open then drove down to the sluggish Yarriambiack Creek to set up camp under the gnarly old gum trees on its banks. The waterway flowed away from the Wimmera River further north eventually emptying into Lake Coorong near Hopetoun.

With her tent erected, sleeping bag unrolled and grateful that restrictions had been lifted so she could set a fire for later tonight, Addie baited the yabby nets and set them in the water. Backed up against a tree trunk, she chewed on a blade of grass, frowning, deep in thought, tilting back her head to watch sunlight sparkling through the sparse foliage overhead.

To her surprise, she must have dozed off, woken by screeching parrots to see her net line pulled tight. Yes! Lunch. She hauled in her first basket of fat blue-green shellfish, dumped them in a bucket of creek water, rebaited the net and tossed it back.

Although she had the ute two way radio, Addie had brought her phone in case Harry made contact and now checked it in case she had missed a text or call. Instead, her heart sank to read yet another *reminder* from Bernie Grant that "*…in the interests of company security, you are advised not to discuss the current situation with anyone.*"

Furious, knowing she didn't care and was about to break their warning with Harry's imminent arrival, Addie emailed back "*Only with my lawyer*" then flicked her phone to silent and focussed on fishing.

Fresh cooked yabbies dipped in vinegar, with scones and a thick lashing of butter for lunch, sent Addie into contented heaven putting her in an easier mood for the forthcoming meeting.

Expecting him to arrive late afternoon, she straightened in her camp chair at the sound of an approaching vehicle much earlier. Whatever he was driving discharged a rumbling purr. Didn't sound like his most likely luxury four wheel drive.

When Harry appeared over the slight rise above the creek, it was astride a gleaming motorbike, clearly tuned to perfection. She sighed with envy. Nice wheels. As for its pleasant sound, working alongside Nick in the farm workshop over the years, Addie knew it all came down to the exhaust.

As for the rider, in normal circumstances he was a person she would not have readily arranged to see but ethics forced her hand and dictated she disregard their history. Although to be honest, even now she knew in her heart she still held a fondness for Harry. But today she was here on principle and to right a wrong. Although she didn't expect it, if he chose to show a little gratitude it would help restore her faith in him after his betrayal.

Doing him this favour in making him aware of potentially impending disaster, Addie hoped to gain more respect from the Chandlers than they had shown her in the past and prove she was impartial.

When Harry legged it off the bike and removed his helmet releasing dark wavy hair flopping every which way as usual, Addie stifled a gasp. Damn. Had he always been this stunning or could a bloke grow more handsome? It had been a while. She noticed his squinted scrutiny was equally focussed on her as his muscled body strode closer, forged into his usual moleskins, fitted pale blue checked shirt with the collar up. His trademark country look. No city suit today.

'Oliver's new toy.' He indicated the machine behind him by way of a conversation opener. 'Asked if I could take it for a ride.'

'Good cover story.'

Okay, so the ice was broken. Once their initial jolt of seeing each other again was over, they fell silent.

Harry planted his big hands on his hips and broke it. 'I was surprised to get your call.'

'I was surprised I made it.'

'Desperate then, huh?'

'If you're not nice to me I have Dad's rifle in the ute.'

Harry threw back his head and laughed. 'It never used to be loaded.'

Addie was caught by surprise that he remembered such a small thing from their childhood. 'Still isn't.'

'Better be important.'

'It is.'

On the one hand, Addie wanted to get down to business, blurt out what had happened but this reunion was proving uncomfortable. Both being wary, it looked like they would need to ease back into each other again. At least their spark of humour was still there.

Playing for time to unwind because they both needed it, Addie turned and led the way toward her campsite, not realising Harry would have a top view of her shapely back end in tight jeans. Once they reached the fire, she indicated for him to take the other camp chair.

Harry scoped out her campsite and nodded toward her camera bag. 'Still taking photos?'

Everyone used their phone these days to snap pictures but Addie never went anywhere without her high end digital camera. 'Keeps me sane.'

He hesitated before asking, 'You in trouble?'

Although it was said with amusement, Addie flinched at the harsh observation. But he was right. She would never have made contact unless forced. 'We both are but I don't scare easily.'

Harry shot her a heavy stare beneath raised eyebrows. She ignored the urge to jump right in to the reason for contacting him after so long.

'How's Austin?'

He eyed her more steadily and Addie even believed she saw those broad shoulders relax. Her strategy was working. His gaze strayed toward the campfire low flames and coals.

'Father's well. We're busy with our companies of course.'

'And Isabelle?'

'Mother loves their social life. She's blossomed since they moved back permanently from the Wimmera to their Albert Park mansion.'

The corners of his mouth twitched with humour.

When she married Austin Chandler, Isabelle came with money. Although she raised her sons in the country, their lives were now firmly based in Melbourne among its exclusive elite in support of their highly successful IT company, Chandler Digital, begun Addie suspected as a career move for their clever younger son, Harry.

'She was born in the city,' Addie graciously acknowledged. 'Only natural. How did Oliver meet his fiancé?'

'Melissa? Around sheep. Literally. Her folks own a big pastoral station down south of Hamilton in the Western District. Live in an historic bluestone homestead that's a warm family home. Melissa's lovely,' he said softly, his gaze drifting away from the fire and back to Addie again. 'A country girl. Natural and bubbly. A perfect fit for Oliver.'

'I'm happy for them. Pass on my congratulations.'

Addie gradually edged toward their other company business. 'The Chandler Foundation has taken off.'

'It's father's baby, really. He's focused on our charitable arm. Exploring how we can bring computer technology to disadvantaged children, starting with our own indigenous communities.'

'It sounds like a fabulous project.'

'Father has handed over Chandler Digital to me.'

'Well done. You're highly successful. Stiff competition for Carlton Ross.'

'Envious?'

'Yes and no.'

Now they were gnawing closer to the bone. Addie had left Melbourne University for Oxford to complete her education. Her girly crush for Harry had weighed her down long enough once she realised he only dated gorgeous society chicks. Not nerds like Addie Kendall. When the truth finally hit home, Addie stung, knowing she wasn't so much out of Harry's league as just not on his radar. Social or otherwise.

But the biggest blow was returning from England years later, highly qualified, older and wiser, yet still being rejected.

'I know that scowl. Spit it out.' Harry sent her a challenging grin.

Even after all this time, wanting to wring his privileged neck and at the same time drawn to him as though no time had passed at all, and there hadn't been a five year gap in communication, Addie sighed. She had missed that breathtaking smile but hesitated to explain. It would sound whiny, like asking Harry to justify her loss, begging for an apology or at least an acknowledgement of their mistake. When back then it had all been about business, if prejudiced, and she didn't expect one anyway.

Kendalls didn't whine. They got on with it. But, hell, she had never shied away from a dare and especially not one from Harry Chandler. Besides, clearing the air couldn't hurt although she obviously needed it more than he did. Wisely she kept her voice low and calm.

'I applied for that contract job with your company in good faith. I didn't expect any favours because you knew me. I offered your father a stunning résumé in an immaculate portfolio. My credentials dripped with brilliance. I was genuinely shocked to be overlooked. You and your father were both on that interview panel. I won't lie. I was deeply hurt to lose.'

'Father had the final say,' he explained.

Addie thought even a younger Harry had more backbone. 'Then I didn't lose to someone more skilled for the job. Austin chose a socially acceptable man over a working class woman.'

'I was as surprised as you.'

'Did you speak up for me?'

'I tried.'

Obviously not hard enough. 'What did he say?'

Harry casually shrugged. 'He hinted at your personality. You are inclined to be blunt.'

'You mean honest.'

'Tactless. And apparently your appearance at the interview-'

'No decision should be based on how a person looks. That's discrimination.'

'It's over and done. Don't argue.'

'I'm not. I'm just explaining why I'm right.'

'Move on, Addie,' Harry teased. 'Father's old school. He probably considered you weren't the right fit for the company. At the time.'

'You mean a disadvantage.' Addie tapped her boot impatiently in the dirt.

'It wouldn't happen these days under my watch,' he guaranteed.

'Pleased to hear it.' Harry seemed to have stepped out from his father's shadow and was his own person now. 'At the time I knew it was pointless to challenge or appeal the decision. I would only have embarrassed myself and your father would never change his mind. I get that life's not always fair but, on paper and in reality, I was the best applicant. I take personal pride in that.'

'Maybe it was for the best,' Harry said gently.

Addie scoffed. 'Don't dress up prejudice as a favour.' She paused, adding wryly, 'I'm here to do you one and possibly save your company.'

Harry sent her a long stare. 'Okay, let's hear it.'

Understandably, he seemed eager to move the conversation forward to the reason for his visit. Only mildly uncomfortable about their past issue and its unfairness. She had said her piece so now at least he knew how she felt.

She shouldn't have let the injustice fester. It was more to do with Harry not fighting in her corner than anything else. Although she supposed he had no reason or personal interest to do so. Then or now.

She was a tomboy nerd. Harry was just plain smart with an old business head on young shoulders. They connected and sparred academically during their later school years. But you couldn't force someone to like you. Back then, less worldly wise, Addie had lived in hope. Talk about pathetic.

Chapter 3

Addie opened the Engel and offered Harry a beer.

His head dipped in a quick nod. 'Still my favourite. You always had a stellar memory.'

Pleased, Addie grabbed one for herself, snapped off the lid and took a swig. When she was seated again, she said quietly, 'I'm taking a forced *leave of absence* from Carlton Ross.'

Harry leaned back, crossed one leg over the other and frowned. 'So what gives?'

'The official version is *I'm working from home.* Actually I don't really mind. Any excuse to escape the city.' She pulled a wry face. 'Except I still have to return to Melbourne for our Section meetings every Monday and face my opponents. A lot of wasted kilometres but at least I can get in and out in a day. The reason?'

Addie took a deep breath and gradually began to explain the evolution of her IT breach discovery, the tense and awkward company meeting that followed, the consequences and her suspicions.

'So, I was the curious employee who stumbled onto an irregularity,' she summed up, 'and as it turns out now, stupidly went to next level management with my concerns, opening a can of worms. My gut tells me it's Morgan himself with an agenda and a secret.' She sighed. 'I could have signed the document they produced. Naturally I didn't but I'll bet the fine print was scary. I was assured I would have full company legal support. As if,' she scoffed, 'because the second I put my signature on any piece of paper with the Carlton Ross letterhead, they would forget I existed.'

Harry bent forward holding his beer, arms resting on his knees, staring at the ground and shaking his head. 'Addie, this information is beyond alarming.'

With a flash of pleasure, she noticed since meeting today, Harry no longer used her childhood nickname like he had during their phone call in the city yesterday. 'It was rather sinister watching the situation unravel before my eyes on the computer screen. I mean, the proof was right there in front of me. I've already seen a lawyer and given her a copy of this.' Addie produced another USB.

'What is it?' Harry held it up.

'Evidence. Up to a point. The whole situation is just not right. And it's too much of a coincidence that it happens to threaten your company, their biggest competitor.'

'Addie I'm so sorry about your circumstances,' he murmured.

She shrugged. 'Thanks but I was planning to move on anyway.'

'No consolation but I'm personally grateful on behalf of my company.'

'I can imagine,' she held his gaze, adding softly, 'and you're welcome.'

He checked his watch. 'I can't stay much longer today but we need to talk more about this.' He glanced around. 'Looks like you've dug in for a few days. I presume you'll still be out here tomorrow?'

She nodded in confirmation. In that moment, it hit Addie just how well she and Harry knew each other. Still. Like his reference to her camping out which they had done as district kids in the school holidays together. Just old habits, or was there more?

'Right.' Harry pushed himself to stand. 'I'll swing by again tomorrow and we'll discuss possible strategies. Meanwhile I'll drag my top security guys away from their weekend to start checking our system and what you found on this little guy.' He waved the USB in the air before attaching it to his keyring.

'You should consider an ethical hacker. Bypass your employees.'

Hands on hips, Harry set down his empty bottle and paced. 'I headed the team that set it up. We update all the time. We should have been fine.' He tossed her a grateful glance. 'But I take your point.'

'Someone from Carlton Ross cracked your code. Maybe they've already tapped into your information, maybe not. Whatever, you need to plug it.'

'I'm well aware of what's at stake,' Harry growled.

Confronted by his sharpness, Addie could see he was frustrated and struggling. As any CEO would at the thought of employee betrayal and a hacking competitor. 'Don't blame the messenger,' she said wryly.

Harry halted and had the grace to look humbled. 'I'm not. I apologise. It's not the breaking in that bugs me. That's serious enough. What I'd like to know is *how* they found out we have anything worth stealing?'

'Your own company leak?' There were crims everywhere.

His heartfelt gaze turned her heart. 'I'd trust you with my life, Addie, and by today's heads up I know we're on the same side. I appreciate you must have been conflicted between our two companies.'

'No conflict. I'm all for right against wrong.'

'Fair enough. When we talk tomorrow we'll go deeper. For now, just so you know since it has a bearing on the breach and the outcome, in confidence?' He raised his eyebrows. She nodded. 'Chandler Digital is in the final stages of a product development potentially worth millions.'

'Something new,' Addie murmured almost to herself. So there was a fortune at stake here then.

'Best not to use our phones,' Harry advised. 'That's why I didn't text you about coming early.'

She shook her head. 'Been taking precautions on that front already.'

'I'll sort out communications between us by tomorrow.' Harry stared out across the campsite toward the creek. 'I should head back. Oliver will be worried about his bike and the family will be wanting help setting up the marquee in the garden.' He turned back, grinning. 'Thanks for the beer.'

Addie rose and didn't know what to do with her hands so she jammed them in her pockets. 'Sounds like it will be a great family night.'

She watched in admiration and with more than a little nostalgia as he clipped on his helmet, settled onto the bike and roared away.

With Harry gone, Addie felt lost, knowing the feeling would pass when they started brainstorming plans tomorrow.

Later, she barbequed sausages and onions washed down with another beer. Enjoyed a flaming autumn sunset and listened to crickets chirping in the grass. There sure was magic in the night by a campfire on the creek. Balm for the soul before her life probably grew more knotty.

Addie whiled away Sunday morning, camera strung round her neck, crunching through the bush and dry grass, taking advantage of the sharp light just after sunrise. Capturing nature and wildlife activity. It had been too long since indulging her photographic eye. Cityscapes didn't hold the same appeal although she had captured many detailed close-ups, sharpening focus on specific features, their backgrounds blurred.

By early afternoon, she felt ridiculously pleased to see Harry again, this time driving his own wheels, a classy four wheel drive. What some country folk jokingly referred to as a city tractor. Not necessary on urban streets and freeways, more a status symbol. Although to be fair, deep down Addie couldn't really believe that was Harry's intention. His more privileged background and natural intelligence sat easily on him.

He was barely out of his vehicle and striding toward her, flashing a smile, when he said, 'Told the family I needed to leave early. I'll return to Melbourne direct from here.'

When he was close enough, he tossed her a small box. 'Prepaid phone. No GPS.'

Addie caught it. 'A beer?'

'Maybe one. Need a clear head for thinking and driving back.'

'Good party?' she asked as they sank into opposite camp chairs before the coals remaining since building a fire for her toast and packet soup lunch.

He nodded. 'Didn't sleep much though.'

'Me either. Wondering how to approach this

and what to do first. I wasn't forced to back off because Carlton Ross care about their staff. Why push me out when they should be using me to plug the leak?'

'Because they already knew about it.'

'Exactly.'

'Don't worry, Addie. I'll take it from here and keep you informed.'

She almost tipped out of her chair with indignation. 'You're not doing this alone!'

Harry reeled in surprise at her fierce reaction. 'You found the evidence now it's up to my company to get to the bottom of it.'

'Not without my help.'

'Honourable but is that wise? Addie, think about it. You could be personally at risk.'

She raised eyebrows of dissent. 'I know that.'

'You're vulnerable and have already been threatened.'

'I can handle myself.'

'I know and I remember the scrapes it used to get you into.'

'Childhood inexperience. I'm a big girl now.'

Harry grinned. 'Of course but-'

'No buts. I understand you need to investigate the Carlton Ross company leak from your side and try to salvage any threat. With tempting big money involved, some people are easily persuaded to step over the line and become informer. But you're not *my* boss.'

The weird thought flashed into her mind that

if she had won that lucrative job at Chandler Digital a few years ago, he would be.

She steadily held his gaze, aware he was not liking what he heard. Ridiculous to think he wouldn't want her pursuing this situation. 'My reputation is on the line. For a different reason I have as much of a stake in this as you. Do whatever you need for your company security but I'm out to not only find the Carlton Ross culprit but why he or she needed to break the law. No way are you leaving me out of this search.'

Harry pushed out a heavy sigh and shook his head, his dark eyes flashing a combination of frustration and respect in her direction. 'All right. But watch your back every step. I won't be around to keep an eye out for you. Judging by their desperate tactics so far, if this crime is critical to Carlton Ross survival, it probably comes down to money.'

'Morgan Ross is wealthy.'

'On the surface.' Harry shrugged. 'Maybe not.'

'You think? Could be just greedy for more.'

'Plenty of people love the smell of the stuff and turn corrupt to get it.'

'Okay so looks like we need to dig into the family background. Starting with Morgan Ross personally. Besides his company, as far as I know, the family still hold the Banyandah homestead block and land the other side of the creek.'

'As it happens,' Harry revealed, 'out of

interest I drove past just before on my way here. Still looks deserted.'

'I wonder why the family no longer use it even as a weekender anymore. It's a fabulous old place but neglected.'

A guilty look crossed Harry's face. 'If my own life is any indication, I imagine too damn busy to take a weekend off.'

Addie noticed it was said with an edge of humour but his comment bothered her and she knew a hint of concern.

'Besides,' Harry went on, 'Morgan never struck me as a country type. His kids, Logan and Kimberly, were educated at private school in the city. After his parents died and that business of his missing older brother, Hudson, the importance of the Ross country estate kind of faded.' He grew thoughtful. 'Might be worth double checking with a local real estate agent though.'

'I can do that,' she offered, 'but if the homestead had been sold there would have been publicity.'

'Probably. The Ross ancestors sure built up an empire but over generations, those vast property holdings become too expensive to run and most land gets sold off.'

'Banyandah was a working property while Hudson was in charge.'

Harry scowled, shaking his head. 'Tragic losing his wife and sons in that road accident. You have to wonder that his disappearance not long after was definitely suspicious.'

'Never to be found.'

'No,' Harry murmured, reflective.

'So with the parents long gone and the oldest son and heir, Hudson, missing, I guess the property has been in limbo.'

'I believe after seven years a missing person can be declared dead.'

'It must be ten years now though so why didn't Morgan sell if they don't use it?'

'The land around the homestead is leased and productive. Maybe they're holding onto it for the property's value increase. After his brother's loss perhaps the heart went out of him.'

Addie scoffed. 'Morgan Ross? Yeah, right.'

'Well a shadow seemed to fall over the Ross family in the district after that misfortune.'

'Let's not get too sentimental. We're after facts and the truth. Don't suppose your IT guys have turned up much yet from the USB?'

Harry slowly shook his head. 'They think it could be a virus that the Carlton Ross hacker planted. Maybe one of our employees innocently opened it but it's all conjecture until we find definite evidence on our system to uncover and link the hacker's identity. When we find some reasons, we might be closer to an answer.'

Addie raised the issue on her mind. 'Don't need details of course but how damaging could it be to your new product if significant data is already taken?'

Harry drained his beer and lounged back in his chair, feet crossed at the ankles. He didn't give the impression of a guy whose entire business was currently under siege.

'Whatever they've taken, if anything, might only be a small part of the product and not totally understood on its own. Only our guys know the full picture so it may not be as useful to them unless they can build something of their own out of it. And that takes time. Our product is virtually market ready. But the pressure is still on to identify the Carlton Ross culprit and extent of any information theft so we can hit them with a legal case.'

'And to do that we need to get behind the Ross family façade.'

'Simple,' Harry grinned.

'Do you intend telling your father about the breach?'

'You're assuming I haven't.'

'I guessed you wouldn't want to spoil a family weekend.'

'True. Probably not, unless news gets out and Austin hears something. The plan is to keep it in-house with only a handful of guys informed. The fewer employees know, the safer and more productive our investigation will be. Not only that, but Carlton Ross mustn't learn we're onto them.' He turned a steady gaze in her direction. 'Which means they'll be watching you, Addie.

Maybe not so much out here but take care in the city tomorrow.'

'Sure.' She was beyond touched by his genuine concern and obvious personal interest. The warm eyes, the gentle voice. He really cared and her heart stirred. But she wouldn't read anything more into it than that.

'For my part,' Harry said, 'I see the Ross family socially so I'll keep my eyes open and ears tuned in to any potentially relevant gossip. At a recent function, I noticed Logan's dating Stephanie Smythe, Kimberley's friend. As a result, apparently she's won a job in the Ross company.'

Addie chewed on that information for a moment. She hadn't heard anything to that effect. Something else Morgan was keeping quiet about.

'I'm not much for girlie chats but I suspect Steph is the vulnerable kind. If I get a chance away from watchful minders, I could ask around tomorrow and see if she's in the building. Accidentally run into her and see what I can learn.'

'Be careful, Addie. I'll call late tomorrow and we'll compare notes.'

After their important shared confidences this weekend in the wake of a five year drought, Addie had no idea how Harry would take his leave. So when he rose, she did too and waited.

He hedged a bit and studied her calmly at length, sinking one hand deep into his pocket and laid the other gently on her bare arm. 'Thanks for everything. We'll keep in contact and see this thing through.'

The effect of his touch worked its way through her whole body. 'Sure.'

Her only consolation as he walked away was knowing she would see him again. But she held no illusions. This new association was strictly business.

As Harry Chandler turned off the gravel road onto the highway for the city, his thoughts flicked back to the gutsy woman he'd just left behind.

The little IT nerd he knew from childhood didn't give an inch back then. This weekend at her creekside camp she was even more self-assured in her simple and mature country way. Jeans, tee shirt and boots. Long blonde hair pulled back into a loose braid and swinging down her back. She'd always been stubborn and independent, holding her own in a family of brothers.

While the dangerous situation to which his company had been exposed would now fully consume all his efforts and time until solved, he found he was looking forward to spending time with Addie too.

She was honest and loyal, had placed her own safety at risk by bringing the current problem to his attention when she really had no need. Just showed the quality and strength of the woman. He was impressed.

With a tinge of guilty regret, he reflected on the bum steer she had been given five years ago at the job interview in his company office when his father still held the reins. Not being in touch in recent years, he hadn't realised how deeply Addie was offended back then. Her principled nature shone through even as a kid and Harry knew it reflected poorly on his family. His father's compassion had softened over the years but the damage had still been done.

He began to brainstorm ideas as to how he could possibly right an old wrong.

After Harry left, Addie grudgingly packed up camp and headed back to the farmhouse. Where possible, with six adult Kendalls all going in different directions these days, Sunday night was usually family time before the week revved up again. Although Nick lived in town, his feet were often under the family kitchen table for meals. Darren manned the patio barbeque while Julie and Addie trotted out bowls of salads and vegetables.

Sitting around together later, everyone chatting, teasing and laughing, out of nowhere Mitch suddenly asked Addie, 'Did you have a visitor over the weekend at the creek?'

Addie froze. 'Why do you ask?'

'Thought I saw a flash of sunlight off a vehicle out there.'

She cringed as she replied, 'I may have moved the ute once or twice.'

'That old thing is so dirty and rusty it wouldn't reflect,' Lachie quipped.

Everyone laughed so Addie let the matter slide in silence. She thought the creek hollow would be safe but it was ingrained in every member of the family to remain alert around the property, even after summer's end with the threat of bushfires still possible before the seasonal breaking rains due soon.

Next morning, always reluctant to leave the farm, Addie didn't head back to the city until sunrise, giving herself enough time to attend the weekly Section meeting at midday.

To avoid distraction and disturb the sense of calm that always settled on her after a relaxing country weekend, Addie turned off her mobile. Until she reached her Fitzroy terrace and garaged Gertie for the day, only one text reminder about the company meeting appeared on her phone.

She had shared a pre-dawn pot of tea with her mother in the farmhouse kitchen. Now she needed breakfast so she scrambled three of the fresh eggs from the farm with fried tomatoes on toast, filled her keep mug with tea and ran for the tram. Another reason she hated the city. Life always seemed to be such a rush and keeping to time. So much more laid back up country.

As she walked back into the historic Carlton Ross building toward the lifts, Addie developed a wary sense of being watched. In her mind, all eyes were cast in her direction. In reality, nobody probably even noticed her in passing. All the same, her gaze flashed in every direction. Didn't hurt to be cautious.

In the meeting, only Addie and Steve Wilson knew an undercurrent between them making her uncomfortable the whole time. Interestingly, it was mentioned that Stephanie Smythe had joined the IT Section as support staff, confirming Harry's comment yesterday. So it was official. Knowing the woman's lack of technical skills in the field, Addie's first thought was what on earth the newcomer would be doing. It occurred to her that Stephanie could be a company plant. No mention of the internal security breach, of course. The boss would keep that little fact hidden. Yet their Section should be the first to know and humming with activity by know.

To her surprise, her future absence was briefly referred to by Steve. 'Addie Kendall will be temporarily working off site on a project.'

That's what they were calling it! At the announcement, James looked across the table and raised his eyebrows.

Later as they were all leaving, he grabbed her arm and whispered, 'What gives?'

'Miss me already?' Addie teased, growing used to not really answering questions anymore.

Steve silently appeared from behind. Had he been listening to her brief exchange with James?

'I need Addie now,' he said pointedly to his subordinate.

'See you next Monday,' Addie said brightly to James.

Steve pulled her aside to the corner of the room. 'Best you leave immediately,' he warned.

Addie needed an excuse to stick around and find Stephanie. 'I'll be collecting a few personal things from my station first.'

'We'll keep you informed of any news.'

'Be a nice change from intimidation but I won't hold my breath.'

Addie turned her back on him and walked away, irritated at yet another subtle threat. She exchanged minimal greetings with her fellow workers but, to her amusement, because he looked so miserable and pathetic, briefly stopped by James' work desk.

'Get a grip, Woodsy. We all have a job to do.'

'How long will you be missing?'

'Till it's done.' She grinned. This deflection business was growing easier every time. 'Tell me, where is Stephanie Smythe working?'

'You have nothing in common with her.'

Addie chuckled. 'True. Just want to say welcome.' James pointed out the location. 'Thanks. See you next week.'

On her way, she grabbed some unnecessary belongings from her desk just for show, shoved them in her bag then headed in Stephanie's direction. Finally, good fortune was shining on her this morning. The blonde was just checking her hair and makeup in a mirror, possibly to head out for lunch. Perfect.

How to work this? Playing it by ear sounded like a plan.

Chapter 4

'Stephanie?' The young woman turned from checking herself in a compact mirror. 'Hi, I'm Addie Kendall, 2IC in Security. Just heard in our weekly meeting you're working for the company now. Welcome to our team.'

Stretching the truth of course. At the moment she was unofficially powerless and suspended but no one in their Section knew that.

'Thank you.' The blonde stood, her smile radiant, her poise confident.

The girl was gorgeous. Long bouncy hair, red nails and fancy clothes. The IT dress code was usually slightly more down market. The poor thing was at risk of being privately ridiculed and only employed courtesy of the Ross family. Logan's trophy girlfriend. Addie's heart wrenched for the woman, knowing she was about to take advantage herself.

'I guess I'll see you around?' Stephanie said hopefully, perhaps desperate for a friendly face.

'Actually I'm working from home at the moment.'

'Don't you live on a farm?'

'Yes. I grew up with Logan and Kimberly until secondary school.'

'He mentioned. I don't think I could ever live inland so far from Melbourne.'

Stephanie made it sound like the Wimmera was on another planet. Addie smiled. 'Millions of people feel the same way but its different growing up in the country. It's what you know and love.' She crossed her fingers and continued. 'Looks like you're off to lunch. I won't hold you up.'

'Oh no,' Stephanie said uncertainly, 'Logie's busy so I was just going to find the company café.'

Logie? Cute. Addie thought quickly. The executives, including Morgan Ross himself, as well as Steve Wilson and Bernie Grant, used their own private dining room on the top levels.

'Really? I was about to grab something light before I leave. I'd be happy to lead the way and maybe join you?' she suggested with a smile.

Stephanie brightened. 'That would be fun.'

Addie wasn't sure about *fun* but it might prove beneficial to her cause. Any small piece of information might be helpful. 'I'll point out some of the IT members so you'll recognise a few faces,' Addie offered in the lift a few moments later, hoping other Section co-workers didn't make or report anything of their lunch together.

'That would be great. First days can be awkward.'

'Where did you work before?'

Stephanie wrinkled her nose. 'Logie has a lawyer friend so I worked in his office for a while.

But that didn't work out,' she brushed it off.

Considering the whole feminine package that was Stephanie Smythe, Addie only hoped it wasn't some kind of workplace harassment. She knew what that looked like now. It could take many forms.

When they were settled at a quiet table in the café and she snacked on a club sandwich, Addie began casually probing. 'Kimberley did a Fine Arts degree didn't she?'

'Yes.' Stephanie stabbed her salad. 'She's really clever. She has her work on exhibit in a gallery at the moment.'

Addie asked for the location, deciding a visit might prove worthwhile. 'What are your own personal interests?'

Stephanie's blue eyes positively glowed with enthusiasm. 'I did a Diploma of Fashion Styling for a year. I love clothes and shopping. I have so many favourite boutiques. I'm always sketching designs,' she said almost apologetically but with a certain boldness.

Addie witnessed her glamour firsthand. Stephanie's style showed the woman sure knew how to put herself together. 'Well, I wish you success.' She edged the chat in a more useful direction. 'If I remember correctly, you and Kimberley are not only good friends but you have birthdays about the same time, too? Around Christmas?'

'Yes. You have a great memory,' she

observed sharply.

This woman was savvy. Surprising she had teamed up with someone as superficial as Logan Ross.

'Both December,' Stephanie added. 'I'm the first and Kim is the fifteenth.'

Addie logged that snippet into her memory as possible future password access options. 'So you've known Logan for quite a few years.'

'I surely have. He's five years older than Kim and I, as you would know, and he was always around but we didn't really connect until recently. Naturally he studied business at university. I know his reputation as a playboy,' she caught Addie's eye and smiled, 'but he seems more focused on his career and the company now. We'll see how it goes. Early days.'

'It's interesting talking to you about the Ross family having briefly grown up with them as kids. Most employees in the company never really get to know who they work for. Thanks for sharing.'

'You're welcome.'

'I won't share this conversation,' Addie confided.

'Thank you. The family appreciate their privacy.'

'Understandable. I imagine people take advantage.'

'Oh, they do,' she agreed.

'Logan's quite a catch,' Addie teased.

'So am I,' she countered with a chuckle, 'but he's just Logie to me. With all his faults.'

'We all have those.'

'He *was* being fast tracked up the company executive ladder and groomed for the Board.'

Addie's attention sharpened. 'That's not happening now?

Stephanie hesitated and finished her glass of wine. 'Logie had *words* with his father recently. He works long hours, travelling all over the country and into Asia. Perhaps some people need an outlet.'

'What kind of outlet?' Addie probed gently.

Stephanie rolled her eyes. 'Gambling. Online casino gaming on his laptop, especially when he's travelling. I've tried to warn him.'

Addie saw a scenario unfolding here. 'So his father considers it a problem?'

'Potentially. I overheard their argument. Morgan did not sound happy but he's been like that lately. Stress of work I guess. His father disapproves because Logie has no anti-virus on his computer. Says it slows down his games.'

'That's a fact,' Addie agreed, alert to a potential weakness. 'It exposes his system.'

'His laptop *is* amazing.' Stephanie sounded impressed. 'A boy toy. It lights up like Christmas. It's a really cool thing to see.'

'I believe I have,' Addie grinned, thinking of her workmate James and his similar leaning toward gaming. Although more responsibly.

'Logan and his father will sort out their differences. The company is hugely successful and I'm sure that always comes first.'

'Absolutely. The Ross family hold a lot of influence.'

'I'm sure they do.'

'It's important for Logan to focus on building his career. Our relationship is steady for now but we're not making any big decisions. I get it, considering the family company is in challenging times at the moment. It's tough out there, right?'

Addie nodded. 'IT and technology is a highly competitive field but would the Ross family even feel hard times?'

Stephanie's blue eyes twinkled. 'Oh yeah. Logie's father is cracking down. Losing his temper. Banning Logie from updating his Mercedes Roadster this year. Poor baby,' she gave an infectious laugh.

'Really?' How the other half lived. That was a six figure vehicle!

Hanging around one mechanic brother and listening to all three enthuse about cars in general, including fantasy machines, Addie got the gist. If she remembered correctly, the sports car Stephanie mentioned had a soft top, deep seats and an interior like an aircraft cockpit. Must make for some exhilarating rides. Logan was always one to impress.

Addie could only imagine. Such a luxury car was beyond the average person's reality. Even if she could afford it, Addie wouldn't buy one. Gertie trundled along just fine. No matter what you drove, you could still only go 100 on the highway so what was the point? Unless you had access to a private racing circuit. Being a Ross, that was entirely possible.

'Morgan bleats about household expenses. Kimberley doesn't care. She's self-sufficient but her mother loves her designer gowns,' Stephanie added.

'With the family being socially prominent, I imagine you attend all kinds of fabulous occasions.'

Stephanie chattered about recent events and galas. It all sounded way beyond anything remotely of interest to Addie. But it did raise the question of why family patriarch, Morgan, felt it necessary to cut costs these days. Not all appeared rosy in the company, a situation she and Harry considered at the weekend.

Addie wondered why and to what extent. Having personally experienced the restrained anger of Morgan Ross' need for utter control recently herself, she itched to know the root of his money problems. Surely not a son overspending on gambling? There must be more. A bigger factor at stake here.

Addie had tuned out of Stephanie's gossipy conversation until she started name dropping which pulled her back to alert in case they were people Harry knew. She memorised them. Maybe they would mean something to him.

To honour her word before leaving, Addie pointed out a few fellow workers in the café that she felt might be more easy going and connect with Stephanie. Addie even mentioned James. Maybe the fashion thing gave them something in common. The woman came across as fun loving but with a sound head on her shoulders. Might be worth keeping in touch on her Monday conference visits because of Stephanie's close association with the Ross family and any valuable news that might help her current search.

On her way out of the building in the early afternoon autumn sunshine and before she forgot them, Addie tapped the society and business names Stephanie had mentioned into her private phone with Harry.

She noticed a text from him. *Trust today's meeting was bearable. Can't meet today as I hoped. Work. Following up leads. Will phone tonight.*

Addie's exhausted spirits rose. It had been an emotionally tiring day so far. Rising before daybreak, driving city bound for four hours, fronting the Section meeting and quizzing Stephanie. She was disappointed not to at least see Harry's friendly face but probably for the best. Morgan Ross might be having her followed so any future city meeting in person would need to be strictly planned. Meanwhile their joint protected mobiles were their main contact and proving effective.

She wanted to be home by dark. With all the Ross company crap being dished out at the moment and until the whole beat up fiasco was resolved, Addie didn't want to be driving alone at night. Especially not on isolated country roads. A foolish fear maybe but nearing the end of her journey as the lowering sun cast long shadows, paranoia had her flicking glances in Gertie's rear mirror. Watching out for any strange vehicles she didn't recognise. Too shiny and clean for country dirt roads.

A white four wheel drive had followed her since the freeway ended an hour ago so Addie stopped off for a leg stretch and, instead of her usual mug of tea, one of Holly's famous coffees at the Coach roadhouse.

The trailing vehicle passed and didn't pull in so although Addie knew a brief respite and sense of relief, even out here she would stay watchful to ease her mind when she continued later.

Before returning to the farm, and checking no vehicles were close as traffic thinned further up country, Addie detoured off the highway and onto the gravelled road that ran past the Ross family's Banyandah homestead.

Barely visible from the road along the avenue of eucalypts leading up to it, Addie stopped at the stone pillared entrance. Oh what the heck. Out of curiosity, she turned and slowly drove in.

As the homestead emerged into view, surrounded and half hidden by grand old peppercorn and gum trees, she thought it such a sad sight and waste to see it desolate and unoccupied.

Years ago when the Ross family were in residence, many social functions and open garden days had been held here. Addie herself had attended one or two and been inside the house. Although the family were on a higher social scale, the Kendall and Ross kids attended the small local district primary school. Until Logan and Kimberley were bundled off to Melbourne private secondary schools. Their uncle Hudson had known tragedy by then and mysteriously vanished.

After that, sightings of the Ross family had stopped.

Feeling cheeky, Addie pulled Gertie around into the front circular driveway and stepped out. In awe, despite being cast in long evening shadows, she glanced up at the beautiful red brick Victorian country house. Its cornerstones were in contrasting cream and encircling veranda decorated with ornate cast iron.

Slowly walking around Addie drew on her memories of the home's happier times. Inside, she knew, the central staircase led to a generous number of bedrooms and bathrooms off broad landings and its huge downstairs hallway opened left and right to vast reception and dining rooms, an extensive historical reference library and spacious kitchen beyond.

Addie rubbed her arms as she strolled around to the rear. And froze. She darted back around the side of the house and slid her mobile from her jeans pocket. How had they not heard her drive up in old Gertie?

Two men both young, one tall with dark messy hair, the other short and dumpy wearing a cap backwards were peering in windows between cupped hands. She recognised neither of them nor their beat up ute.

She quietly snapped photos of the car and licence plate on her camera phone then paused to see if she could hear any of their low conversation. But she was too far away and dared not move closer or reveal herself at this shadowy time of day out here alone with two strangers.

She could hardly challenge them about trespassing when she was doing the same thing. Except she was a local and although you couldn't know everyone in the district, somehow Addie suspected these guys weren't.

She hiked fast back to her car, cringed as she started the motor, planted her foot and sped away. She didn't notice the men following as Gertie laid dust down the long driveway. Being unique, her old Holden was easily recognised.

Her heart only slowed its pounding when she was sure the men weren't in pursuit. Oddly, they sent out untrustworthy vibes. Judgemental on appearances, she knew, but it wouldn't hurt to show her photos to Ewan Holt, one of the local policemen who played footy with her brother, Lachie.

After a typical and reassuring warm Kendall welcome following her unsettling encounter at the homestead, Addie slipped back in among her family for a late dinner. Heartening at the end of her long demanding day.

Because Harry had promised to phone, Addie kept both mobiles in her pocket. Not long after dinner, he called, so she excused herself, seeking the privacy of her room and closing the door.

'Sorry to be calling late,' he apologised. 'Been a mad day all round.'

'No problem. Everything okay in your company?' She settled into her comfy chair, one foot tucked beneath her, wrapped in one of her mother's lacy crocheted shawls. The open window admitted a fresh night breeze. Hearing Harry's voice, Addie suddenly didn't feel so tired anymore.

'Yeah, the IT guys are working above and beyond. Thoroughly checking all our systems.' When he paused, Addie thought she heard a stifled yawn. 'Nothing yet though. What about you? Any leads on anything?'

'Nothing concrete. Possibilities. Most interesting one is Stephanie Smythe working in our IT Section now.' Addie filled him in on details of her café lunch conversation. 'Could be coincidence. Or not. I'm bushed tonight but I'll try the dates she gave me for passwords to get into the Carlton Ross computers.'

'I heard a rumour a while back from both business and social contacts, that Morgan Ross was scrambling for cash. Companies often seek private investors but there might be something in it. I'll keep probing and see if I can learn anything more.'

'I noted Stephanie's work computer address so if I can't hack in, I might start sending fake emails to her with links. See if she takes the bait and clicks on any. I know it's dodgy but it's the simplest way to access their company system at the moment. Steve has me on a tight leash when I'm in the building. I have to assume he's watching my every move.'

Addie detailed her close encounter with the intruders at Banyandah earlier. 'Might be nothing but I'll mention it to Ewan. See if he thinks it's worth following up. And I'll contact some local real estate agents about any possible whispers of a sale on the homestead property.'

'Keeping yourself busy,' Harry paused. 'You doing okay?'

'I'll be fine.'

'Not what I asked,' he chuckled. She melted a little at the deep earthy sound. 'I'll keep in touch. Take care.'

'I will. Night.'

Addie held the mobile against her chest, eyes closed, long after the call ended.

The next day did not start well. A text was waiting on her mobile when Addie woke up. *About yesterday. Next time go straight home. Lunch with a family contact looks suspicious.*

How? Addie fumed. Who the hell saw and blabbed? And the nerve of the company accusing *her* of shady behaviour. To burn off her lingering steam straight after breakfast, Addie jumped in Gertie and sped into town.

She sat in the car by the river and phoned around estate agents. After the third call, she was interested but not surprised to learn that the Banyandah homestead property had recently been quietly placed on the market for private sale by tender. Apparently with private viewing only, no open house inspections and no advertising. Not unusual then that no one had heard about it.

In the circumstances, Morgan Ross wouldn't seek publicity for his reasons behind the sale. Unless they had deep pockets, prospective buyers would take one look at the rundown property and leave. After the sale, the big country house would take another fortune to restore. Few farming locals had that kind of spare money. Addie didn't like Ross' chances of selling any time soon. Large estates often sat on the market for months, a year or even longer. If strapped for cash, Addie guessed Morgan wouldn't want that.

She couldn't fathom how even a remote historic million dollar property would make any impact in reducing such a wealthy man's debt. A man like Ross would need much more. Millions.

The burning question on Addie's mind now was why Morgan's fortune had changed? How could he lose it all or be in such a tight spot he was forced to sell off assets and break the law to stay afloat? For she was convinced he was personally behind the Chandler Digital hacking. Thanks to their squatter pastoral ancestors, Addie wondered if Logan's gambling habit was an emotional response to a potential Ross company downfall. He and Kimberley had been raised amid wealth and had never known any other lifestyle.

Absorbed by the news and its wider implications for a while, Addie finally started Gertie again and drove to the police station. Fortunately Ewan Holt was on duty.

'Don't usually see you during the week,' he said.

The observant cop coming to the fore. So, yet again, Addie explained away her work situation then showed him her photos, admitting she was trespassing herself.

'I understand the property is for sale but the two blokes didn't look like potential buyers to me,' Addie shrugged. 'Might be nothing. Just sticky beaks.'

'I'll check it out.' Ewan eyed her closely, grinning. 'What were you doing out there?'

'Just being a concerned neighbour and taking the scenic way home,' she shot back with a smile.

'Keep up the good work then.'

'I intend to. Later.'

Ewan was single. His muscles strained against that flattering blue policeman's shirt. He sure looked powerful in uniform. He was fun but no chemistry. And cops tended to transfer and move on.

Addie sighed as she strode from the building. She was a Wimmera girl born and bred. If she ever found that elusive special man he would need to be an established local. Country men were scarce and in demand. By her age now, most were partnered or married and possibly kids.

The truth and direction of her thoughts hit home for Addie and stung. Maybe she was better off in the city. Too much time to think out here and she had only been home a few days.

That night after setting up the links, feeling guilt and deceit as she did so, Addie began her email blitz to Stephanie. Waiting was agony and she felt her mother watching, wondering why her daughter was hardly working. It bothered her to mislead her own family. If, not when, the Ross family troubles and the truth came to light, she could explain to those she loved.

It didn't bear consideration that she might fail. It was too late to go back and change the events following what she found and reported on a routine IT security check in the Carlton Ross office that day. But her obsession to find the truth would drive her on.

Every day for the rest of the week, Addie sent off simple innocent looking emails to Stephanie's office computer. With no reaction. The woman was either busy or smarter than she looked. She even tried variations of the birthdays as passwords to crack the system and sneak in.

She took breaks out on the motorbike, losing herself in the freedom of fresh air, under sunny skies, the gravel roads between stubble paddocks kicking up a trail of her ramblings. Always with a camera slung around her neck or tucked away in the saddlebag to capture that elusive perfect image moment. The daily excursions on the open roads or in the bush along the creek impressing on her how much she loved this country. And how she wanted to combine her work and life here.

Sometimes she swung by the hollow where she had camped and the water was deepest, pulling off her helmet to brave the muddy creek water and stripping down to her underwear for a dip while the weather remained mild. Wondering how long this searching process would take. Telling herself to be patient. Not an attribute she possessed. Uncertain where her future lay now and whether she was able to prove her innocence.

The alternative didn't bear consideration.

Chapter 5

One evening, Addie was out later than usual photographing sunsets and riding home just after dark. She was on the boundary road between Kendall land and the Ross property when she thought she noticed flashing lights in the distance through the trees around Banyandah homestead.

When she looked again there was nothing. She considered the risks going over there alone at this late hour and hesitated. If the two dodgy men were back and up to no good again, clearly something fishy was happening. Since she was on the motorbike, the prowlers would see and hear her coming so she would lose the element of stealth to investigate.

By the time she went home and returned with one of her brothers to go over there and check it out, they might be gone. So, this time, Addie backed off, weary from losing sleep and working late on her efforts to crack back into the Carlton Ross system.

Maybe she had only imagined the lights.

In the coming days, her frustration moved to impatience that Stephanie had not yet taken the email bait. She worked at night, sending more bogus links, knowing if there was no positive result soon she would need to find another way in.

Her work mate, James, immediately came to mind but aside from the problem of asking him if he would even be prepared to become involved, there was a complication if he was discovered. Like losing his job. Addie would never ask that of anyone especially such a good friend.

If she could just access the company network, a whole world of technical storage data would open up for her. She could trace any Chandler Digital files which carried their own identification, proving someone from inside the Carlton Ross company stole their rival's information. At least then she could pass them onto Harry and he would know the extent of the cyber-attack.

Addie set aside the laptop on her bed, stretched and wandered into the kitchen for another mug of tea.

Her mother was still awake, reading in her favourite chair. 'Not going well, dear?' Julie looked up from her rural fiction novel, her favourite genre.

'It's a challenging assignment.' Not a lie. Just for her own personal investigation not the company.

'I hope your incredible salary is worth it.'

Addie was beginning to question that herself.

In one way, the following Monday morning came too soon and yet not soon enough. Leaving four hours early for the city office was a necessary grind, making her realise the inconvenience and seriousness of her present changed work circumstances.

The Section meeting proved tedious since Steve Wilson drew her aside beforehand advising that she was no longer allowed input. What was the point of her being there?

Alarm bells rang for Addie to be further removed from having any authority in decisions whatsoever and her voice effectively silenced. Her future here was looking dimmer and less likely each day.

'The boss expects you in his office immediately after this meeting before you leave town,' Wilson added in an arrogant tone.

Addie could only imagine *that* meeting definitely wouldn't be helpful to her in any way but felt pleased she had arrived early and slipped James her note before Wilson appeared.

Honestly, she felt like walking out. Regardless, she listened carefully to everything discussed and closely watched all team member dynamics with each other for any clues of collusion.

Nothing seemed obvious so, instantly the meeting ended, Addie was on her feet, deliberately passing James close.

'See you next week?' she murmured.

'I'd like it to be sooner.'

At which Addie smiled because it meant he

had read her note. 'I wish,' she quipped, confirming she understood.

With Steve glowering at them from a distance across the conference table, Addie turned her back on him and strode out to the lifts. He was beside her in seconds.

Because Wilson was a condescending weasel, she despised the man and had nothing to say, she chose to remain silent all the way to Morgan Ross' office. Likewise, Steve ignored her, texting on his phone while Addie reflected on the reason for this summons to the boss.

Morgan didn't rise when they entered his sanctum. Nice.

Addie remained standing. 'I assume this won't take long since you will be keen for me to leave Melbourne as soon as possible.'

Morgan glanced up from between furrowed brows, clearly unimpressed by her nerve and muttered, 'Please yourself.'

The gloves were off. Addie prepared for the worst.

A wad of paperwork was laid out on the desk before him. One by one he turned them around. She scanned them from a distance, reading the words *Termination of Employment*.

Always a possibility in the back of her mind but within ten days? They really wanted her gone and out of the way. For keeps. She was definitely a serious threat then. Pressure from inside the company must be growing intense.

But exactly who were they protecting?

All things considered, she was best out of it. But Addie knew her rights so she took up the papers and found a seat on Morgan's padded leather sofa to read every single word. At her leisure. Twice.

All the while, no one spoke, the only sound slow ticking from the old mechanical clock on the wall behind Ross. It must drive him nuts. Yeah, it was obviously a special piece of machinery. Her mechanic brother Nick would appreciate it but, personally, Addie preferred the sounds of the bush.

Occasionally she paused in her reading as if considering the document on her lap but instead let her gaze wander over the massive pieces of contemporary art hanging on the walls. Fascinated why anyone considered them valuable.

The upshot of the paperwork between Carlton Ross and Adrianna May Kendall was a termination of employment contract, paid out in full in lieu of notice, with immediate effect.

Her sharp brain for figures analysed their detailed final offer without fault.

On the last remaining sheet of company letterhead was a prepared letter of her acceptance carefully worded with plenty of space to sign. Presumptuous of them for sure but Addie acknowledged they were all agreed on this process and the outcome.

She took a deep breath, rose from her comfortable seat and stood once more in front of Morgan Ross.

'Since I've been released from my contract to be paid out in full and I know I've been a loyal and conscientious employee, I presume your reasons are along the lines of *secret company business.*'

She had no intention of objecting to their request or threatening to sue. Addie intended to put her energy to far better use elsewhere. Perhaps they believed a payoff for the matter at stake here would be dropped by her and forgotten. If so, they had seriously underestimated her and were all about to be mistaken.

'The final payout is already in your bank account,' Morgan said smoothly.

'I should expect so. May I see the transaction?' He showed her a printout. 'I'll just make a phone call to my bank to verify.' She pulled out her mobile. When the deposit was confirmed, she said, 'That's a beautiful pen. May I?'

Morgan handed it to her, she signed both the original and copy documents, kept one for herself and stepped back. She waved the pen at him. 'I'll just keep this as a souvenir.'

The steam from Morgan's nose and ears was almost visible. 'Wilson,' he barked, his lackey's cue to kick her out.

The malevolent last glare from Morgan before she walked away, head held high, was chilling. She might be out of their employ but not out of their sights.

With nothing more to lose and officially detached from the company, Addie defiantly decided to take a chance detour before returning to her terrace. Which she would now need to pack up. Another contract to terminate. Her lease.

It was certainly turning out to be a day for endings.

Changing her thoughts to a more positive direction, Addie also realised this was an opportunity for a fresh new beginning. Except right at this moment she didn't have a clue exactly what.

In the letdown following her work termination, and emotionally drained, Addie left the Carlton Ross building for the last time and stood on the pavement, feeling lost. She couldn't face public transport so she decided to blow her budget and grab a taxi to South Yarra, one of many creative art hubs in the city.

At the gallery, she paid the driver and took a deep breath before entering. There was a high chance Kimberley wouldn't be in attendance but Addie wanted to see the work of the most independent member of the Ross family. While the only Ross daughter kept her artistic career separate from Carlton Ross company business, her connections had possibly helped in her success. Kimberley was always the brighter star and far more grounded than her wild older brother.

As the glass doors slid open and Abbie stepped through into the spacious light filled rooms, she knew that if this visit achieved nothing else, it would be to learn a little more about the Ross family member she had known in childhood. Based on Stephanie's revelations, Kimberley must surely be aware of, if not privy to, the family's current financial situation.

Addie's research so far had yielded an impressive list of personal career credentials for the young woman. Her work was already sought by private collectors while she also held lectures and workshops, attending exhibitions and festivals all over the world.

Noting the healthy prices displayed beside each painting and large number of red dot sold stickers as she strolled, Addie understood Kimberley Ross was well placed to afford the life she had built in her own right, regardless of her wealthy background. So any financial fall in the Ross fortune would probably not unduly affect her.

Addie admired Kimberley's natural talented style. The peaceful atmosphere among the other mostly silent browsers in the gallery, with only the occasional murmur, helped her unwind from her recent confronting appointment with the artist's father.

Although she preferred tea, as she inhaled, strong coffee aromas drifted across her senses. She glanced toward the rear of the gallery space to see where it was coming from and noticed not only a self-serve café area but also the artist herself.

Not missing this opportunity, Addie moved toward Kimberley as she was ending a conversation with an elderly gentleman wearing crumpled clothes, a beret and a cravat. Clearly an artistic associate.

As the man left and Addie approached, Kimberley recognised her and smiled, casually elegant in fitted jeans, an oversized shirt and boots, her hair caught up in a messy bun at the back.

'Addie Kendall. What a lovely surprise.'

'I heard about your solo exhibition from Stephanie.'

'Oh that's right, she works for the company now. Logan's influence I imagine.' She checked an impressively sparkling wrist watch. 'You here in your lunch hour?'

'No. I've just been terminated from Carlton Ross,' she announced carefully. Kim's eyebrows rose, her expression genuine surprise. 'Wasn't given any reason,' Addie shrugged, 'but there seem to be internal issues.'

She watched her one-time childhood friend's look of horror as she reached out and laid a hand on Addie's arm. 'Addie. I'm so sorry. After years with the company, I'm shocked to hear that.'

At least one family member gave a toss. She decided to push it. Nothing to lose, although she fudged her own background situation. 'Me too. Downsizing? I've heard money problems?'

Kimberley rubbed her arms and folded them, frowning. 'I've never been interested in the holy dollar. Much to my parents' disgust, I've stayed right away from the company business. But father has been making noises lately, yelling at people on the phone. More than usual,' she said wryly.

Addie found it hard to believe the composed and gracious woman standing opposite was any offspring of Morgan Ross.

'So there might be something in it,' Kimberley continued. 'Mother says the purse strings have been pulled tighter on the home front.' She shrugged. 'Doesn't really affect me. I wear all my clothes more than once,' she chuckled.

Addie's opinion of Kimberley had never changed. She was still delightful and unaffected.

'I understand father was refinancing a new project. Trouble with banks and investors. Happens all the time. I'm sure he'll push through it again as usual. Like every other IT competitor I guess.' She sighed. 'The very reason I've kept my distance from that world. I see what it does to a family and I want nothing to do with it.'

Kimberley shrugged as she continued. 'But some people are driven. Born to be competitive.

Logan isn't, so heaven knows what lies ahead for the family business if he ever takes the reins. To be honest, I don't feel his heart is in it. As you know,' she flashed a grin, 'he loves the high life but he's not cut out to work for it himself. It's a shame.

'Father has worked himself hard to build the company. To be honest I'm surprised he chose IT. As well as business studies at university way back when,' she flicked a smile, 'father studied Fine Arts. Once we moved to the city and because I already loved art myself, he took me along when he visited art galleries and exhibitions. He has an instinct for art investment and trends so it was exciting for a teenager like me to tag along when he bid on a work at auction. He's built up quite a collection in the basement at *The Gables*.'

'I noticed some contemporary art in his office today when he was signing away my fate. Not my preference.'

Kimberley's mouth twisted wryly. 'No. He bought those based on the artist's growing reputation. Mother hates them but father says they're an investment.'

'Really?' Addie wasn't convinced. 'I much prefer your own unique nature landscapes. They're huge canvasses and I love the clouds. Maybe I can afford you one day,' she grinned.

'I've always dabbled with paint. The one thing father and I have in common. Not much else though, I'm afraid,' Kim said sadly. 'All of our worlds were rocked when Aunt Alexandra and the boys were taken in that horrible accident and Uncle Hudson disappeared. His whole family loved that Wimmera property. Afterwards, father closed up Banyandah. I suspect because he couldn't face returning to where his brother and family used to live. As far as I know, he's never been back.

'Ever since, he has shut down from our family and driven himself to be successful in business. A bit like his own father, my grandfather, Ben. I don't remember him very clearly,' Kimberley frowned, 'but apparently he was a tough old bugger.'

Addie idly reflected on Kimberley's disclosure about her father. Perhaps he wouldn't have become such a tyrant if he had followed his passion for art. Another separate personality born out of tragedy and loss maybe.

Yet his father, Ben, had been hard so it was also likely Morgan had inherited a similar character. When you dug deeper into families, it often proved surprising and was unfair to be judgemental without all the facts.

In the light of what Kimberley told her, Addie's opinion of Morgan Ross, based purely on her own experience, had been challenged and slightly tempered but she still had a company breach to explore and would hold her final judgement until that hunt was complete. She decided to mention that Banyandah was quietly up for sale.

Once more, Kimberley was surprised. 'Really? Well, probably time I guess. With Uncle Hudson gone, it makes sense in father's current financial difficulties.' She wrinkled her nose. 'All the same it will be a pity to see the ancestral home leave the Ross family though. I have great memories of growing up out there in the country.'

'Yeah. Seems like another lifetime huh?'

'It surely does.'

'Well, I hope Carlton Ross survives. These days nothing is guaranteed, especially in the IT business.'

'Absolutely. Even running a small concern of my own is demanding. So how are your parents and those handsome brothers?' Kimberley changed the conversation.

'Seems Lachie might actually have a serious girlfriend. Nick's living in town, still climbing under trucks, cars and machinery. Mitch is the same quiet country boy. Mum and Dad are both fine.'

'Glad to hear it.' She hesitated. 'You going home then?'

Addie shrugged. 'Yep. No place else I want to be at the moment. Need to consider my options now.'

'Whatever you do, best of luck with it. You were always the smartest kid at school.'

'Thanks.' Addie glanced around the gallery. 'Your talent is obvious too. You're a success already.'

'Just doing what I love.'

'It shows. Nice to chat. Later.'

Outside on the pavement, waiting for a taxi, Addie contemplated her conversation with Kimberley who confirmed her father's money woes and probable reasons for desperation. She would be heartless if she didn't take on board the personal double misfortune around the family in the past. But it still didn't change the present fact that Morgan Ross was ambitious and clearly not above corruption to survive.

Which only led Addie to wonder what else he had done over the years to claw his way to the top.

Chapter 6

As Addie rode back to her terrace in another cab, she instructed the driver to drop her off in the lane that ran along the back. That way she could unlock the garage to start loading Gertie with extra belongings she might need in the coming weeks at home on the farm.

Before she left the city today, she needed to walk down to Brunswick Street and have her house re-let by her real estate agent. There would be a fee but they would have no trouble finding another tenant. Addie could see no reason to keep her rental terrace. She had no idea where her next employment would be. Once the Carlton Ross hacking issue was resolved, she could focus on her future work position and choices.

Addie unlatched the wooden gate and headed for the back door, still preoccupied about today's events. The key in her hand was already halfway to the lock when she noticed the door ajar, alerting her to a possible break in or the equally nasty alternative that Morgan Ross had sent in a spy.

Either way, furious, and never one to stand back, preferring to confront situations, Addie whipped out her mobile, dialled 000 as she flung the door wide and barged into her tiny kitchen-laundry.

'Harry!'

She swiftly cancelled her emergency call.

With a look of surprise and amusement on his face, he raised his hands in the air. He wore a cap pulled down low over his forehead that looked ridiculous with his suit. 'Not armed.'

But dangerously handsome. 'What are you doing here?' Her heart slowly reduced its pounding.

'I'm undercover. I was careful. My driver dropped me off in the lane,' he said.

'How did you find where I live?'

'I have sources.'

'Of course you do,' she said wryly. 'You could have sent me a warning text and saved me the fright.'

'This was much more fun, wasn't it?'

What was wrong with him? So light hearted for a man whose company secrets were in jeopardy. On reflection, more like the child Harry had once been before he became focused and successful. Not ambitious, just using his natural gifts of a sharp business and analytical mind to his advantage.

'For you. How long have you been waiting?' Jammed up close in the small space, Addie stayed put near the door.

'A while. Thought you'd be back sooner.'

'How did you get in?'

'Muscle.' His mouth twitched and he crossed his arms.

Addie wasn't sure whether to consider Harry's surprise visit as a treat or a complication. She had hoped to cram as much as possible into Gertie's boot and head for home by dark after her other expected visitor arrived.

Harry eased the tension Addie didn't realise she felt when he strolled off into the narrow passage running the length of the deep house on its narrow block.

'Hope you don't mind but I checked out your photograph walls. Quite an impressive portfolio. How did that develop?'

Addie groaned. 'Your wit hasn't improved.'

'I mean, I know you always had a camera with you as a kid but how did this urban monochrome style come about?'

Addie followed him, aware there wasn't much more space in the hall than back in the kitchen. It was fine for one person but two meant you better be friendly. Harry removed his cap and ran a hand through his hair, peering keenly at her works.

Addie grew embarrassed. 'I take them for my own pleasure really.'

He tapped on a couple of them. 'The black and whites and close ups are a perfect reflection of hidden gems in every corner of the city. You have a keen eye.'

'Thanks.'

'When do you find time?'

'I make time. It's an attitude. That makes a difference. Besides,' she admitted, 'it's vital to my sanity in a noisy city. When you see light on something no matter how small or notice a unique image, it turns the world to mute while you study and capture it.'

She grew self-conscious beneath Harry's intense gaze while she spoke.

'You have technical and artistic talents.'

'I guess so.' Forgetting her hospitality with his sudden appearance, she asked, 'Can I offer you anything? A drink?'

'Don't want to hold you up but a big mug of strong black tea would be great.' He glanced back toward the kitchen and then in the opposite direction down the hall toward the front door. 'Do we stand or is there some place to sit?' he teased.

'Very funny.' She pulled a face. 'There's a sitting room up front. Make yourself comfortable. I'll bring down a tray.'

When she arrived a short time later, Harry had removed his suit coat and tie, his legs sprawled out in front, crossed at the ankles, fully relaxed as was his style on her small two person sofa.

After setting the tray on the table between them with their tea mugs and a packet of hastily opened bought biscuits, Addie sat opposite on the only other single chair in the room. She assumed he had come for a catch up chat. Seeing him again after a week was beyond pleasant. Reassuring.

'Help yourself,' she offered. 'I don't keep much food on hand now I'm leaving.'

'Yeah, that's why I called before you head home.'

She had to start telling people sometime. 'No, I mean I'm leaving for good. I'm letting the terrace go.' She paused because it was going to sound awful. 'My contract with Carlton Ross has been terminated.'

Harry sat up and edged forward in his seat. 'Damn Addie, that stinks. You okay?'

His expression was soft enough to be disarming. She nodded. 'That's why I was later getting back here. Took a cab ride. Gave me time to calm down and think. Deep down maybe Morgan Ross did me a favour,' she muttered. 'I'm not a city chick. Blue skies and wide wheat plains are in my blood and more my style. Perhaps I shouldn't have persevered and stayed so long.' She smiled weakly. 'I can start again.'

'You shouldn't have to,' he said darkly.

'Maybe I want to.'

They shared a long gaze.

Harry broke it. 'You have been so wronged in all this.'

'I'll get him. I can wait. How's your own company situation?'

'We're monitoring our system 24/7 for any

hint of further infiltration. You?'

Addie shook her head. 'Stephanie still hasn't clicked on any links. Annoying. But on my long way back from the office earlier I stopped by Kimberley Ross' exhibition at the gallery. Just to unwind really after my dismissal. I didn't expect it but Kimberley was there in person and we had a chat. She's still lovely and natural as I remember from school. Was really open and forthcoming about her father. Ross is definitely in financial trouble.' Addie explained the gist of that conversation.

'So if his company is poorly managed and he's shy of investors, he's in a serious place,' Harry said, 'and if he's developing new technology like us, it takes time to come on the market. My guess is he failed through lack of resources so he's looking in my direction for big money to speed things up. By the way, I received your text about the homestead sale but a million won't be nearly enough to dig him out of a hole.'

'Exactly.' Addie's mood lightened with inspiration. 'So if Banyandah is up for sale, as the only surviving family member, Morgan must have inherited the property after his brother disappeared. So why were those blokes snooping around the property? Frankly, they didn't look like the brightest stars in the sky but they were definitely casing out the place. For themselves, or are they working for someone else? Being unoccupied for years, there can't be much left inside. Unless the two guys don't know anything, aren't connected at all to Morgan Ross and were just taking a punt seeing what they could find?'

'It's all a mystery at the moment. A few dots still need connecting but the facts will all come out eventually.'

Addie finished her tea and set down her mug, reaching out for a biscuit. 'It's still too much coincidence though. The mess Ross is in and suspicious activity at the family homestead. I live nearby so I'll keep an eye on it.'

Harry glared at her. 'Be careful. You don't know the extent of what we're dealing with yet.'

Addie loved that he said *we*. 'True, but once I tap into the Carlton Ross computers and track the intruders over at the house, we'll know more.'

'I don't like the idea.'

'I'll be fine.'

'No expeditions after dark, okay?' he warned.

'What if I see activity again?'

'You won't if you're not there.'

She scoffed. 'How are we supposed to learn more if we don't go looking?' From Harry's disapproving scowl, she noted his fading tolerance.

'Addie this is serious.'

She gave a thumbs up. 'Check.'

'Don't do anything alone until I get there.'

Addie sat up straighter. This was news. 'Where?'

'The farm.'

'Yours or mine?'

'I'll be staying with Oliver and Melissa.'

Harry Chandler sure knew how to spring a surprise. 'When?'

'Sooner rather than later by the sound of it.'

He was coming because he thought she was in danger? 'For how long?'

'Until the job's done.'

'Indefinitely? How's that going to work running your company?'

'I trust my staff. I'm a phone call away.'

A speechless Addie shook her head and took a moment to absorb what Harry was saying. 'It's not necessary you know.'

'I disagree.'

He would. 'You going to chain us together or what? You can't be with me every minute.' Breathtaking thought all the same.

'I'll be ten minutes away instead of four hours. I'll sleep better.'

'Your decision, but all sounds over the top to me.'

'Thanks, Harry.' He pulled a wry face and rose.

Addie had the grace to at least cringe slightly inside. Her big mouth had caused offence again. She just couldn't believe Harry would interrupt his city life to be out here with her.

She stood to face him. 'I'm not ungrateful,' she murmured. 'Sounds like overkill until I actually find out what the homestead intruders are up to or I can crack the Carlton Ross network.'

'Listen to yourself,' Harry said, reaching for his coat and tie slung over the end of the sofa. 'You're talking as though you're in this alone. I'm involved here too. I want to be *with* you,' he emphasised. 'Addie, you found the leak and informed against your own employer to tell me my company's data security is at risk. Big time. Now you've been unfairly sacked. On both fronts, there's a lot at stake. Your reputation and Chandler Digital. It might be worth millions but a human life is priceless. I intend to help you every step of the way, okay?'

Quite a sermon. Addie folded her arms, her tough tomboy image cracking to hear such soft heartfelt words spoken in her favour. By the very man she had always admired. 'Fine. Accepted.'

Addie knew she sounded ungracious but she was finding Harry's position unbelievably kind and therefore overwhelming. Plus trying to wrap her head around his stance on moving back home to the Wimmera. For her safety, as he claimed, but surely also for his own peace of mind that Chandler Digital would ultimately be safe when she learned exactly what files had possibly been stolen from his company and the outcome of the homestead activities.

In that regard, they both needed to keep their private mission quiet. Ross must never get wind of their efforts to prove his guilt and expose him.

Harry was leaving the room so Addie followed. As they stood awkwardly together in silence, they heard a knock on the front door. She knew who it would be and tensed, hoping he hadn't been seen.

'Excuse me,' she brushed past Harry to open it. 'Hi James. Come on in.'

She quickly drew him indoors, her newcomer wide eyed to see who was standing beyond them.

Addie managed to half turn to Harry. 'This is my work colleague, James Wood. James this is-'

'I know who you are.' James' hand shot out and Harry shook it. 'Harry Chandler. An honour to meet you, sir.'

He grinned with amusement. 'Harry will do just fine.'

When he glanced between James and Addie with puzzled interest, she realised he was assessing James as possibly more than a work colleague. If only he knew. She would tell him. Eventually.

'Harry's just leaving.'

He pointed down the hall. 'I'll leave the same way I broke in, shall I? See you soon,' he said quietly but not before a moment's hesitation, then he was gone.

'I can't believe you grew up with that man,' James said in awe as Addie ushered him into the sitting room. 'He's, like, the guru of the IT industry.'

'He's done well.'

'He leads the field!' James took up a place on the sofa Harry had just vacated, arms stretched out along the back. 'So, why am I here?'

Addie slowly perched on the edge of the other chair again. 'I have something I need to tell you and a risky favour I'd like you to consider.'

'You couldn't tell me at the office?'

'Absolutely not.'

'Fire away then.'

Addie privately groaned at his ironic choice of words. She gradually outlined the events of the past two weeks; her security breach findings by the Carlton Ross company against Chandler Digital, and today's biggie, her sacking. During which James' expression grew from interest to astonishment then outrage.

'The bastards.'

'Exactly, but what can you do?'

'Are you okay, honey?'

'That's what Harry asked, too.' She sighed. 'I'll be fine. Eventually.'

'God, darling, there's been no whiff of this back at the office.'

'It's a no brainer as to why not. They broke the law and I found them out. What will you tell them if they've had you followed?'

James shrugged and waved an arm. 'Darling, after what you've just told me, I don't give a damn. After you, I'm the best tech guy they've got. If I walk, I'll bet I can take half the IT team with me.'

Addie gasped. 'You wouldn't!'

'Watch me.'

She sat back in her chair, brimming with delight. 'That would leave them in a mess.'

'Uh huh. Now, what was that favour?'

'Not afraid to ask now. And you can probably guess.'

'You need me to nose around, see what I can find?'

Addie nodded. 'I'll wait a few days longer. See if I can still somehow break in via Stephanie so that will give you a chance to think about what I've asked.'

'Okay. I'll think about.' James tapped his chin, stared at the ornate plaster ceiling rose, looked back down at her and said, 'Thought about it. I'm in.'

Addie shook her head and laughed, then grew serious again. 'You know, you're probably the best and only true friend I've had here in the city.'

'We clicked, darling, yeah?' He nodded toward the hallway. 'Looks like you also have someone else with influence fighting in your corner,' he murmured, acknowledging Harry's recent presence.

Addie shrugged off his curiosity. 'He's an old friend from back home. I'd love to show you our farm one day.'

'Darling, I don't leave the city. I'd get dust on my Nota's. Send me pictures.'

'Coward.' She had a thought. 'Speaking of pictures. If you want any of my framed photos in the hallway, take them. Save me packing them up and taking them home.'

James leapt to his feet, enthused over them and took four. 'You're a dark horse. Harry Chandler in your back pocket and these photographs are fabulous.'

Addie smiled. 'I'll keep in touch if I need that favour.'

They hugged and, in a waft of something that smelt both floral and citrus, he was gone. True friends came in all guises, Addie reflected. None more so than James Woods. She only hoped she didn't need his help, yet equally knew she didn't want Stephanie to be compromised. Addie was already processing ideas on that front.

Running shy of time to leave the city, she phoned her real estate agent about re-letting her terrace and the genuine reasons for breaking the lease. Receiving a sympathetic and positive response, she continued packing up enough possessions to fill Gertie's boot. The terrace had come furnished so she would only need one more trip for the rest of her things.

Addie left the city behind just ahead of the evening peak hour rush. Stopping once for fuel, she arrived at the farm on dusk. A bittersweet homecoming because now her dilemma was confiding to her folks the happenings in her life these past few weeks. But she would need to choose her moment and didn't feel quite ready.

Entering the farmhouse, Addie paused on the back porch step before bracing herself to summon a smile and plod wearily into the kitchen.

'Here she is,' her mother said, back turned at the sink. 'Saw you drive in.'

'Hey Mum.' She kissed her on the cheek.

'Only gone for the day and you've had a visitor.'

'Oh?' Addie leant back against the bench.

'Senior Sergeant Ewan Holt.'

She played the conversation cautiously. 'What did he want?'

'Didn't say. Can't be too important. When I told him you'd be back tonight, he said he'd catch up with you tomorrow. Not been speeding on the highway?' Julie chuckled.

'In Gertie? Good one. I'll phone in the morning,' she shrugged it off.

After a rowdy evening meal with everyone home, the boys migrated out under the patio around the brazier for man cave chat and beers. Her father disappeared into his office so Addie enjoyed some girl time with her mother watching a movie Paperback Hero, about a truck driver who wrote romance novels.

'That Hugh Jackman's a bit gorgeous, isn't he?' Julie said as they strolled down the passage to their bedrooms later.

'You thinking of leaving Dad?' Addie teased.

'You can answer that one yourself.' She chuckled. 'Night dear.'

'Night Mum.'

First thing in the morning, Addie phoned Ewan Holt. 'Hi, Sarge. What's up?'

'Miss Kendall,' he said warmly. 'An update for you on the vehicle and licence you gave us last week. Ute was reported stolen a few days earlier from down south then found abandoned and burnt out.'

'No leads then but suspicious activity, yeah?'

'For sure. We'll check the incident in our system. See if it matches anything.'

Didn't sound hopeful. 'So, nothing you can do at the moment?'

'Not without more evidence or a break and enter. We receive lots of trespass reports from farmers about isolated sheds and barns on country properties. Most pass unseen. Oh, and Addie?'

'Yes?'

'We phoned the homestead owners.' Addie's interest sharpened. This should prove interesting. 'Name of,' he paused, perhaps checking, 'Morgan Ross. Didn't sound too concerned. Got the impression he was too busy to care or follow it up.'

Naturally. Morgan's apathy could be a diversion for the police so they didn't follow up the suspicious activity around the homestead. Put them off the trail of whatever was still important inside.

Addie was beginning to think the two useless guys weren't quite so dumb after all. Their visit was planned.

And, somehow, Banyandah figured in everything happening in the Morgan Ross company right now. There was simply too much coincidence to be ignored.

Chapter 7

Frustrated on many fronts, Addie returned to the farm. With the menfolk out working, amply supplied with full lunch boxes, and after a cosy soup lunch with her mother, she disappeared on the motorbike for another photographic afternoon. She chose to leave her computer mission time until the evenings. Except for a few security guards and cleaners, human presence in the Carlton Ross company office was scarce and her access attempts, if successful, were less likely to be monitored, detected or reported.

While she was out in the north paddock, Harry phoned. 'I'm back home at Oliver's.'

Intrigued to hear him call the Wimmera *home*, she said, 'I've been working at night but I'm afraid I'm still not in.'

'You must be fed up.'

'No need to be so polite. I'm grumpy.'

'How about I come over? Two heads and all that. What time?' He didn't allow her time to object.

Addie knew her mother would disown any member of the family who didn't invite a guest for dinner. So she did and Harry readily accepted. Later, she warned her mother, 'Harry will be here for a project we're working on together, okay?'

'Of course, dear.' She glanced at her daughter in surprise. 'I thought you both worked for rival companies?'

Thinking quickly, Addie said, 'It's a mutual scheme.'

'Companies do that?'

'If it's to our joint advantage, yes, absolutely,' Addie said, as casually as she could muster, all the while thinking she should just tell her family the whole sorry mess and be done with it. Including the fact that she actually didn't work for anyone at the moment. But it just didn't feel right. Yet. Or perhaps, with so much else on her mind, she simply wasn't ready.

Harry arrived just on approaching dusk wearing blue jeans and a black tee shirt. He stepped from his shiny four wheel drive backed by a stunning vibrant autumn sunset. Addie surveyed the whole package and thought *smokin'*. No matter what age did to him, he would remain arresting and handsome without even trying. But then she had always thought him so and nothing over the years had changed her mind.

Julie Kendall had fussed in preparation all afternoon with Harry warmly hugged before he was barely in the kitchen. 'How's your family? City folk now.'

Harry half smiled. 'Afraid so. That's where the digital business is. So Oliver's happily running *Woodlands*.'

'Wonderful news about his engagement.'

'Yes. Melissa's a country girl. They'll crack on fine together.'

Harry settled back in among the family like old times. With five males all country born and bred all seated around the kitchen table, conversation never flagged.

Naturally they analysed the weather, breeding stud sheep and current prices, Oliver's wedding, apparently planned for early spring, and the prospects for another cropping season.

Harry ribbed Lachie about Jenny Campbell.

Her easy going oldest brother didn't turn a hair. 'She's a theatre sister at the hospital. On duty tonight.'

'You might have a fellow nurse in the fold, Julie,' Harry teased.

'She'd be most welcome. What about your own prospects?' she flashed back, grinning, eyes twinkling.

'Working on it.'

To Addie, it sounded like some fortunate female was possibly in the background of his thoughts, if not his life. Which was news to her because Harry had already mentioned he didn't have much time for romance, although she knew his social life must present opportunities.

'Plenty of city girls to choose from,' Darren Kendall quipped.

'True.'

As always, Harry Chandler was annoyingly

evasive. The kind of bloke who sat back and watched everyone else which, as a teen, she had found fascinating yet irritating.

Addie considered casual entertaining the most pleasurable downtime no matter whose company she shared. But particularly tonight, with Harry's added presence right beside her. She was always eager to learn more about him since his absence from their lives in recent years.

So she sat back listening, aware of his occasional side glances in her direction but there was only so much socialising before she grew restless. Especially at the moment with significant work to be done.

Trying to hurry him up without appearing rude, keen to get back to her efforts, Addie waited for a pause in the general conversation. 'I'll go ahead and start work without you, shall I?' she hinted eventually.

Heading toward her room, her father asked, 'Where are you going?'

'To work.'

'Not really enough space in there for two, is there?'

Addie wondered if her Dad was bothered by the fact that Harry and his daughter would be in her bedroom with the door shut. She didn't mind at all but understood the sense in working at a desk. They both had laptops and needed to spread out.

'You'd be more comfortable in the office. I'll

just go clear up in there and you two can use it for as long as you need.'

'Thanks, Dad. Appreciate it.'

Addie had been wondering how Harry would handle all the pastel girly colours in her bedroom that her mother had great joy creating for a daughter following the birth of three sons. Since leaving school and living in Melbourne and London for years, Addie hadn't the heart to suggest changing it, so the bedroom was still as she knew it growing up. Based in the city, she only visited occasionally for weekends anyway so didn't make a fuss. The fact that it gave her mother such pleasure all those years ago was what mattered most.

So by the time Addie retrieved her laptop, Harry had brought his out and joined her in the farm office. They pulled up chairs on either side of her father's desk facing each other and began.

When Harry linked his hands behind his head, Addie booted up her computer and reluctantly admitted, 'My skills have deserted me in cracking Stephanie's Carlton Ross office password. I'm spitting chips I'm not into their company files yet. I need to change direction and think sideways.'

'I'm an ideas and business man. I leave the tech stuff to you,' Harry admitted.

Addie regarded him a moment, mildly flattered, then said, 'On the surface, I believe Stephanie Smythe hides a simpler woman beneath but her background is rich and indulged. Her world seems to revolve around Logan. I haven't explored that aspect yet but she's a romantic at heart so the password might be connected to him.'

Recalling Stephanie's casual reference to her boyfriend as Logie during their lunch office chat, she frowned and started tapping yet more variations of possible password options into the Carlton Ross portal, barely aware of Harry seated opposite, absorbed on either his laptop or mobile.

It took fifteen minutes but suddenly her laptop screen cleared her through to Carlton Ross. Catching her breath after weeks of trying, Addie gasped. 'I don't believe it. I'm in!'

Her hands shook as she half covered her face in disbelief, staring across the desk and shaking her head at Harry. She alone knew how much this moment personally meant but his soft answering expression revealed he understood.

Witnessing her rising emotions, he rose and moved around the desk to give her a hug. 'Well done you.'

Startled by the gesture yet filled with heated awareness, a self-conscious Addie hesitantly pulled away from the muscles she felt under her hands on that tee shirt, his transmitted body warmth on this cool evening and a spicy aftershave.

'Spending time chatting to Stephanie in the office café that day seeking password clues was not wasted after all because the answer was right there in our conversation.'

Now the task ahead was searching for data and files with the Chandler Digital signature.

Harry wheeled his office chair around beside Addie. Their joint excitement was short lived and their hopes dashed as she soon realised that Stephanie's computer only had restricted access and would not allow her deeper into the company system.

On a high one minute and sunk into disappointment the next, Addie wanted to scream. 'They've no doubt deliberately done this against a determined and resourceful ex-employee. Although to be fair the block could be because Stephanie's a new employee.'

She felt nothing but humiliation to have Harry sitting right beside her, to get in and then be barred. They had come so close.

He placed a hand over hers. 'There's always another way.'

That simple encouragement was the nudge Addie needed. 'Just proves Morgan Ross is taking drastic measures to protect himself,' she muttered. 'We'll outwit that thief.'

'Cold comfort, I guess, but it's taken me all of five years to bring my own new idea into reality,' Harry offered.

'Really?'

He winked. 'Some things are worth waiting for.'

Spoken so softly, their shoulders touching, Addie's personal frustration stirred over the sense they had just shared a *moment*. Then her phone rang. Talk about timing. She didn't know whether to feel pleased or annoyed.

Seeing the name come up on her mobile screen, Addie said, 'It's James. I should take this.'

She excused herself and stepped out onto the veranda, dimly lit from the office. She still felt uneasy about imposing on James' friendship but the depth of his loyalty was proved when he agreed.

'James, your timing is priceless. We hacked in. Finally. Only to encounter a lock out.'

'We?'

'Harry's with me.'

'Nice for some,' he murmured.

Addie could imagine his wicked smile. 'James, focus.'

'So you need me.'

'I'll always need you. You're indispensable.'

Suddenly all business, James asked, 'At your laptop now?'

'Will be in a sec.' Addie turned back into the office to find Harry staring at her. 'James is going to try,' she whispered to him.

'Since I have clearance, I can hack in from my own laptop here at the apartment to the Carlton Ross office system,' James said.

'Wish I'd kept going with my search that day when I first saw the breach, before I reported it.

Because then they fired me and I had no more access or opportunity to investigate further. Good luck.'

'Darling, I can only try. Hook into my niceness and let's do this. We both know there are back doors. May take a while. Grab a coffee. I'll phone you back.'

After Addie ended her call, Harry said, 'You know James well.'

He would only have heard one side of the conversation with their usual friendly banter. 'We've worked together for years. In a detached city, he became my bestie.'

'That's how relationships start. Friends first.'

Addie chuckled. 'James is already sorted. He has a partner, Michael.' She gave that gem a moment to sink in.

'Ah.' Harry looked foolish to be enlightened.

'I thought you might have guessed. That's the reason James and I hit it off. No pressure. He's even offered to quit Carlton Ross and come work with me if I want. That nearly wrecked me,' Addie admitted, struggling with her emotions, her challenging life situation at the moment taking its toll.

'There are always a few special people who enter our lives and become important.'

Why did Addie get the feeling tonight some deeper meaning lay behind Harry's every word? It wasn't so much what he said but the intense and almost vulnerable way he voiced them.

'And we're all the richer for them,' she agreed.

In a fitting moment, the subject of their conversation chose to call back on Addie's mobile.

'James.' She snatched it up. 'I have you on speaker so Harry can listen. Good news?'

'Darling, the best.' Addie wasn't sure she could take the suspense. 'Found the location of your detection point and followed the trail through their system. Which is what you would have done. Strange though.' He paused. 'The connection point is Logan.'

Harry glanced at Addie in surprise. 'Why would he undermine his father's company?'

'Stephanie mentioned a gambling habit. To cover his debts maybe?'

'Weird one for sure,' James agreed. 'I'm in the process of downloading all the Chandler files now. I'll send them shortly.'

Addie was almost afraid to ask. 'Does it look nasty?'

'You know what, I'd say recoverable.'

'James, thank you from both of us. You've saved my name and Harry's company.'

'You're welcome. But I can't believe Logan would stoop so low and do something like this.'

'They'll trace your work activity from tonight and know you've found the link,' Addie warned with concern.

'On it. Writing my resignation as we speak.'

'James,' Harry leaned forward and entered the conversation, 'I know you've worked with Addie and your allegiance is understandably to her,' he held her gaze in the office as he spoke, 'but feel free to seek us out at Chandler Digital any time. Send any résumé directly and personally to me.' He paused. 'You'd be part of a small highly-skilled team.'

'He'd love that,' Addie whispered. 'You're his idol.'

'I heard that, darling. Awkward! Well, Harry, doesn't that just make tonight's work all the sweeter,' James gushed.

'Forget loyalty to me,' Addie urged. 'Not sure what I'm doing yet anyway and, besides, Harry will probably pay you more.' She paused. 'James-' Overcome with relief, Addie couldn't continue.

'I know, darling.'

After he hung up, Addie transferred over all the data and files James recovered to Harry's cloud system. She had been operating on adrenalin but, following the evening's proceedings, she suddenly felt overcome with anticlimax. When her eyes grew watery with relief, she wandered out onto the veranda, arms crossed, leaning against a post. Her good name would be cleared and she could move on. But to what? The whole experience had left her feeling adrift and she had neither the time nor the energy to give much thought to her future.

It wasn't long of course before Harry

inevitably joined her, resting a friendly hand on her shoulder. 'You okay?'

'Sure.' She hesitated. 'That was a generous offer you made to James. Be prepared because the esteem and respect he holds for you means he'll probably personally deliver his résumé to your office tomorrow.'

'Addie, I didn't mean to-'

'It's all right. I have nothing to offer him anytime soon. He's pretty damn smart. He won't be unemployed for long. His talent will be snapped up. Now we have the proof of theft by Carlton Ross, I can start to think about my own future. Whatever I do it will be in the country. Between London and Melbourne, I've lived in cities for almost ten years. Since moving back home, even for a few weeks, I'm done with any metropolis. Whereas James doesn't move off paved streets.'

'He doesn't know what he's missing out here.'

'City people often don't.' She glanced up at him. 'Do you ever miss the Wimmera?'

'Have to admit but, yes, the more time I spend back here I'm beginning to realise I do.'

Addie was more than surprised to hear it. 'In this digital age, we can pretty much work remotely from anywhere. That's what I'm planning. Except not sure exactly what.'

'You're so skilled in IT. Pity to waste that talent.'

Addie was slightly bruised that Harry should be so firm and presumptuous with where her future lay. She acknowledged that there was far more opportunity for IT advancement in the city but that was not the place of her heart like the Wimmera.

So with more bite than she intended, she said, 'My IT experience might be set aside for a while but it will never be wasted.' She turned her back on him and began moving indoors. 'Did you want to explore the extent of those files Carlton Ross stole from you?' she asked, not waiting for his reply.

Clearly judging her sensitive mood, Harry tactfully offered, 'I won't keep you from your family. I'll check it all out back at *Woodlands*. Forward it into the office to my team and they can set about restoring and securing the digital footprint of our product. At the least, it looks like they tried to build a picture of exactly what we designed. This proof now also means we know the exact profile of the theft so we can more accurately lodge our law suit against Carlton Ross and its value in damages. It confirms a definite crime. Next step is for a judge to decide the appropriate penalty.'

Harry closed down his laptop and hesitated at the office door before leaving. 'All this means I'll need to have a private conference with my father. Only a handful of people in the company were trusted with the knowledge of the breach so

I want him to hear it from me in person. Means I'll need to go back to Melbourne for a few days for meetings. I'll return when I can.'

'That would be nice but I guess there's no real need any more, is there?' Addie knew it sounded blunt but he would be returning to his world and the sooner they cut ties again, the better her foolish heart would heal again.

'There's still the homestead connection.'

Addie shrugged. 'It may mean nothing.'

Harry was clearly surprised by her change in attitude as to its importance in the whole Carlton Ross saga. 'Well, I should head off.' He ran his spare hand over his weary face, looking exhausted but relieved. 'I'll say goodnight to your folks on the way out.'

Still he delayed near the closed office door, clearly with more to say. 'You know, Addie, getting that proof tonight of the source for the Carlton Ross hacking has saved my company and its future.' He hitched his laptop higher under one arm and sank his other hand into his pocket. 'I'll never be able to repay you for being so honest with me in coming forward to inform against the company you worked for. Proving what you originally found exonerates you of any guilt.'

'Yes, it's a huge relief,' she admitted more kindly.

'I'm disgusted at Logan's ethics though. Wouldn't have believed it of the kid. He had to know there was a huge danger in committing such a crime. I guess he figured the risk was worth it. He'll cause a complete loss of face in Carlton Ross throughout the industry.'

'When I made my discovery that day and reported it, it was obvious they already knew there was a breach. I could see Morgan's fear that day of being sprung. When they're slapped with your law suit, their worst nightmare will come true.'

'They'll have a few more sleepless nights before we put our case together.'

'I guess it's time now to tell my parents.'

'Go you,' he murmured. 'They'll be horrified what you've gone through and totally supportive. My company is behind you every step of the way until the legal ends are tied up. Good luck.'

Without warning, he gently reached out one arm and pulled her against him for another hug, at the same time brushing a brief soft kiss over her cheek that stirred her blood anew. Just when she was trying to distance her emotions before he left her life again.

Addie hovered while Harry took his leave of the family then walked him out to his vehicle in the yard.

'I'll be in touch.'

She nodded, his powerful vehicle hummed into life, the tyres crunched on the gravel and he drove away. She had no idea when he might return but he always took a part of her with him.

What a night, Addie sighed. Good, bad and challenging.

And it wasn't over yet.

Chapter 8

Once Harry left, it was still reasonably early so Addie watched his vehicle tail lights disappear down the driveway and turn onto the road before she returned indoors for the inevitable chat with her parents she was finally able to face.

Lachie had already retired for the night to his semi-bachelor digs in a renovated workman's hut across the yard, just beyond the farmhouse fence, where the wind notoriously rushed through a line of old pine trees.

In the lounge, Dave was hidden behind newspapers, Julie engrossed in a novel and her brothers more or less watching television. Surprisingly, Nick hadn't yet returned to his house in town. Addie's reappearance barely rated attention.

She sank into a free chair across from the flickering warmth of the open fire. 'I have something I need to share with you all. When you're ready.'

Dave's paper lowered, Julie looked over the top of her reading glasses and closed her book.

'Turn it off, Nicko,' Mitch urged. 'It's rubbish anyway.'

'Wait till the programme's finished,' Addie

protested.

'Nah, doesn't matter. Just can't be bothered heading back to town yet.' Nick flicked it off. 'What's up, sis?'

The Kendalls weren't known for raised voices and noise. Perhaps inherited or observed from their patriarch, Dave, always in the background quietly watching and listening. He had now folded his newspaper and set it aside, giving his daughter the courtesy of his sole attention. The family followed his lead.

With her audience listening, Addie gradually launched into the events of recent weeks, explaining the hacking technicalities as best she could for a father and youngest brother whose interest in modern technology stopped at running their farming business on computer. Yet every adult in the house owned a mobile phone. Only Nick indulged in some social media and its distractions for his garage business.

When Addie came to the revelation of the identity of the culprit behind the hacking breach, her dismissal and the threat to Chandler Digital, the room grew thick with expletives.

'Mongrel,' Mitch growled, always his favourite word in such situations.

'Bloody bastard,' Nick muttered.

Addie hid most of a grin. She loved her brothers' raw honesty. Although she noticed her father frown at the cursing, he didn't comment because he may not have voiced it but she was sure had similar thoughts.

'Logan Ross?' Julie said indignantly. 'The cheek of that young man. With all their money, owning a big company and the Banyandah property up here? Wanting even more? And doing that to my daughter and Harry's company? Now that's what I find hard to believe. Although your grandparents had little time for Morgan's father, old Ben Ross. Hard man apparently. Sons obviously inherited some of that crusty personality in their genes. Except for poor Hudson and his family, of course.' She paused in reflection. 'Now there's another mystery from the past on top of all this current scandal.'

Her mother as always came out with the most positive and prophetic conclusions. 'At least you know who your true friends are now. James sounds like an intelligent wag. And although you could have done without the upheaval to complicate your life, at least it broke the Chandler-Kendall drought. That Harry's father was behind the snub to your qualifications was a slur on our family as well. At least the man could have explained the reasons for not giving you that job.'

'Austin Chandler was always full of himself,' Dave said. 'Bit of a softie but somehow he made *Woodlands* into one of the top Merino studs in the district and the country. Oliver loves farming. The property will continue to thrive under his management. Sounds like young Harry has done them all proud, too.' He turned to his only daughter. 'Your mother and I are always here for you, Adrianna.'

'I know, Dad. After tonight, the source of the hacking is finally identified and my professional reputation saved but not legally resolved yet. That will take longer. I might have a chat to my lawyer, Jade, and see what she recommends about unfair dismissal and compensation. Although, to be fair, they did pay out my contract if only to keep me at a distance and cover up their crime. Harry's dealing with his own company law suit of course. Meanwhile,' she let out a sigh of resignation, 'I'll try to figure out what next.'

It wasn't Addie's imagination that she received warmer hugs and goodnights than usual, finally sinking beneath her pink floral doona, thinking tomorrow would be a day off. She would do absolutely nothing. Then her active mind ticked over. Except new bedlinen and a lick of a more neutral paint in her room wouldn't go astray. Her treat. But she would check with her mother first.

She woke long after daylight to find Julie had already left a note that she was in town shopping. At a loose end after breakfast, Addie baked and took fresh warm buttered scones with a farmer-sized slice of cheese on top with a big thermos of tea to her father, Lachie and Mitch in the machinery shed, checking over their equipment ahead of cropping once the weather broke and the first autumn rains fell.

Rowdy and Bandit raced across the yard to greet her. The kelpie, her father's dog, was her favourite.

'Wanna come for a walk later, Bandit, huh?' She fondly roughed him up. Rowdy wouldn't be jealous. He never left Lachie's side. 'That okay, Dad?'

'Of course.'

A long walk across the paddock to the creek with a camera slung around her neck proved reflective and calming for Addie. Bandit raced off at random, nosing out more information about his surroundings. While she snapped close-ups of tree bark, feathery grasses, wildlife and water reflections, the ideas for her future flowed more clearly to mind.

Using her two biggest loves of IT and photography made sense but she was beginning to consider creating two businesses and generate income from each. Regarding her photography, she already had James in her corner as her champion and a chat to Kimberley Ross, already an established name in the art world, would surely prove helpful with suggestions in getting started.

Which all meant websites to build and establishing a social media presence for each. Striding back toward the farmhouse, freshly energised with purpose, Addie grew keen to make a start, no longer distracted by the hacking issue and her job loss. Perhaps she would explore renting or buying a small property in town to live independently again off the farm, as she must.

So the afternoon passed in a drive, compliments of Gertie as usual, calling into real estate agents to investigate available townhouses and becoming inspired over paint colours at the hardware store to invigorate her old room. She grabbed a few samples of greens for the walls that reminded her of the bush and a creamy white on the ceiling to reflect light. Not that she might be around on the farm much longer to enjoy it but it would be a handy overnight room to crash in the future.

Always at the back of Addie's mind, too, was Stephanie Smythe and what might possibly be her wasted fashion design talent. Depending on whether her relationship with Logan survived, the woman might appreciate another outlet to claim her attention. Forge more independence perhaps and step outside the mess about to dismantle the Ross empire.

Being involved by association with Logan in the Ross family, she was sure going to need a distraction after the hacking scandal broke. A few leaked words and the media would be all over it like hounds nosing out the true story. Addie hoped they did because knowing the depth of crime and potential millions Carlton Ross had stood to profit if she hadn't picked up the corruption, Harry's company would have been seriously compromised.

A harsh judgement, she knew. By association, the whole disaster would be devastating for every member of the Ross family and their close connections. Reputations would be tarnished, if not destroyed. Careers blown and jobs on the line. There was a mountain of fallout to come. So many lives would be disrupted and shattered.

In particular, Addie thought of Logan, without his father's company as his meal ticket. With the young man's royal tastes, the path ahead for the only privileged son and favoured child would prove a nightmare or, at the least, a timely wakeup call.

That night after dinner, instinct drew Addie outdoors into the crisp starry night, her gaze inevitably drawn to the east and the neighbouring Banyandah homestead. Invisible from where she stood and perhaps her imagination was too active but she was convinced she saw tiny flickering distant lights in that direction again. Were the two dodgy blokes back? Her curiosity flared. It might be nothing or something. This time, she didn't even try to resist the temptation to investigate.

She only hesitated a second before tucking a small torch into her pocket and jumping on the motorbike. She cut the vehicle headlight and, at a short distance from the homestead, wheeled it among the shelter of trees. Guided by flashing reflected lights, she crept closer. A dark van was pulled up around the back and the same two men were breaking the door lock to gain access into the house.

Once they had disappeared inside and crouching low, Addie followed. Keeping at a distance and out of their sight, she entered the house and waited in the rear porch, hearing gravelly murmured voices to her right in the direction of the kitchen passage on the other side of the staircase.

She edged further along to the corner where the entrance foyer on the other side of the house opened up. A broad space with no cover. So she stayed put.

Were they simple thieves casing out the house?

Then heard impatience in one of the voices. 'We need to find the cellar. The boss said they're onto us so we need to get the job done fast.'

They were in the right area but obviously hadn't either found or seen the steps leading down to it nearby.

The other man, more rational, said, 'We need to know the layout of this place first. The quickest way in and out with the goods.'

Addie wondered what goods when the homestead was mostly empty.

The first man spoke again. 'If not we don't get paid. We gotta get this right. It's more money than we've ever seen.'

The other man sounded disgusted. 'Of course we'll find it, get it into the van and meet up as planned.'

'Yeah. Far away from here. Man, this better be worth it. I don't like the thought of it.'

The men began flashing their lights everywhere, presumably scouring their surroundings, so Addie backed up into the shadows further from sight. As she did her boot crunched on something. She froze.

'What was that?' one said.

She heard the other utter a cruel laugh. 'Out here in the middle of nowhere? You've seen the dust and droppings in this place. Get a grip, man.'

When the burglars' lights and footsteps came closer, with no time to think or waste, Addie took a deep breath and a risk. With her heart pounding stronger, she whirled around, seeking somewhere to hide. She peered around the half open door of the closest room. Although the house was almost in darkness, she couldn't make out any furniture left behind that might provide a hiding place. There was only the thick velvet drapes at the windows, partly open, allowing in a thin stream of light. Across an open space.

Keeping to the bookcase-lined wall, she edged into what she remembered as the grand study, shuffling her way around. When she reached them, she stepped softly in behind the curtains, musty and thick with dust. She pinched her nose between two fingers against a threatening sneeze.

Just in time, for the men moved out from the kitchen passageway into the front of the house and around into the hallway she had just left.

The man who sounded most in charge said, 'We know the layout and the distance from the back door. Next time we need bolt cutters for that rusty cellar door padlock and a garbage bag.'

'Then we're done?' from the other man.

'Keep cool, man, and do as I say. If you don't panic, we'll be fine.'

'We should have done the job tonight.'

'He didn't give us enough information so we don't have the goddam tools you shit. Stop whingeing and let's get out of here.'

Addie pressed herself harder and flatter against the wall, unsure in the darkness behind the heavy curtains if her boots were fully hidden or if the men had yet passed by this room.

She hardly dared to breathe, listening for the slightest noise alerting her to their movements. In the silence, she eventually heard the back door open and shut. Some moments later, the van started up and when the sound of its engine faded, she inched out from behind the drapes and stole across to a rear window.

The van was gone. She dashed to the front sitting room to see their red tail lights halfway down the long driveway heading for the road. Only then knowing it was safe to leave, she stretched, rolled her neck to ease the tension and, flicking on her torch again, moved back through the house, shutting the damaged back door firmly behind her as the men had left it.

The men hadn't said when they would return. Who knew when that might be? It could be later tonight or tomorrow. Daylight or dark. She guessed after dark since twice now that had been their habit.

As Addie strode in the thin shaft of light from her torch across the overgrown rear gardens toward the tree break where she hid the motorbike, she heard scrambling noises coming from one of the nearby outbuildings.

She froze. Were the men doing the job tonight? Had one of them stayed behind while the other went to collect the gear? She hadn't considered that so all of her senses kicked into life and strained to alert.

She listened again and definitely heard what sounded like shuffling off to her left. It seemed to be coming from a small timber shed. Addie may have ignored the situation if she hadn't also heard a soft groan, as though someone or something was in pain or difficulty.

Her every good sense told her to be wary. Hadn't she faced enough adventure for one night? But if a living creature was in trouble, and she suspected it was human, she would never abandon them.

Addie cautiously turned and moved toward

the building. Its broken-hinged door sagged, ajar. She pushed it wider and flashed her torch around inside, wondering who or what she might find or disturb.

'Is anyone there?'

More scraping but no response. The movement seemed to be coming from the back of the shed so she stepped further in that direction over stacks of timber and old gardening tools. Huddled behind the pile, a dark shape came into view. When she shone her torch into the face, the woman seated on forgotten bales of hay stared up at her.

Addie didn't know who was the most surprised but, despite the intervening years since leaving school, she instantly recognised the person. The same wild short and curly black hair, although now with a streak of purple, dark eyes and olive skin reflected her distant Aboriginal background.

'Piper Thorne! What on earth are you doing here?'

'Resting. And…hiding I guess.'

'Who from?'

'Can't say.'

'Fair enough.'

'Please don't tell anyone I'm here.'

'Okay.' Addie noticed blood on her leg. 'Are you all right?'

'It's not serious. I was deliberately run off the road by another car.'

Addie gasped, horrified. 'That should be reported! Did you get the rego? If you describe the vehicle, we can tell Ewan Holt and he'll trace them.'

'No! I'll be fine in a day or so.'

Addie hesitated to ask since it really seemed rather obvious. 'Are you in trouble?'

'I've done nothing wrong,' Piper insisted defensively. 'The guy who ran me into the table drain was following, trying to scare me.'

'Why?'

'Thinking I'll give up.'

'On what?'

Piper shook her head and, despite her predicament, managed a twisted grin. 'Addie Kendall, honestly, you haven't changed a bit. Talk about twenty questions. All you need to know is that I haven't broken the law and I'm sorting out a family problem.'

'Can I help?'

Piper was adamant. 'No. It's complicated. I thought if I hid for a day or so it would give my leg a chance to heal. Besides, if the guy comes back, he won't find me or the car. He'll think I've gone.'

'Where's your car now?'

'Hidden in the bush.'

'So it can still be driven?'

Piper nodded. 'But not far. It's been damaged on the side from the crunch. Something's out of whack. Think it's the right front wheel. I knew the homestead was nearby and empty so I decided to rest here until I can move again. Thought I'd be safe and alone until I saw the van.'

'Yes, I saw lights so I came over to investigate. Did you see them?'

'No, I hid here in the shed. Didn't want to be seen or recognised.'

So Piper would be ignorant of the homestead burglary that had just taken place. 'Only trespassers. They've gone now. Being the nearest neighbours, we keep an eye out.' Not quite true but Addie felt the need to explain.

'I'm surprised the house is still deserted. Must be tied up legally since the family was killed and the husband disappeared.'

'Actually I believe the homestead has just been put up for private sale. I guess with all the publicity when Hudson Ross died they want to keep a low profile through the process. You have to wonder who would buy even such a grand homestead like this with its unfortunate history. Listen, Pip,' Addie reverted to her friend's nickname from school, 'I came over on a motorbike. Are you sure you don't want to jump on the back and I'll take you to our place so Mum can take a look at your leg?'

'No!'

Piper spoke with such desperation, Addie said quickly, 'Okay but at least let me bring back some first aid supplies to dress that wound.'

'Your mother will know its missing.'

Addie chuckled. 'Trust me, with Mum being a district nurse for decades, her emergency first aid box is loaded. And food,' she added. 'I'll bring back food.'

'Oh, I remember your mother's food.' Piper sighed, more relaxed now.

'Yeah, from all those birthday parties on the farm when we were kids.' Addie paused. 'I was sorry to hear your grandmother died recently. Is that why you're back?'

Addie didn't imagine Piper's renewed distress. Her face went blank and she grew silent but eventually nodded.

So Addie moved on. 'I'll be back soon. Actually, do you have a mobile?' Remaining silent, Piper nodded again. 'Could you keep watch till I get back? Those guys have trespassed before. I've already reported it to Ewan Holt. I don't suppose we could swap phone numbers and if the men return, you could text me?'

Piper hesitated, a suspicious expression clouding her face so Addie jumped in to reassure her. 'Promise I'll delete you as a contact as soon as you leave.'

It took a moment but Piper eventually agreed and they exchanged numbers before Addie left.

On the ride to the farm and back, Addie's brain ticked into overdrive as to why anyone was stalking Piper and why they would want to harm her. Whatever the problem, it was definitely serious. She wasn't comfortable leaving Piper anywhere near the homestead where more trouble potentially loomed.

Within twenty minutes she returned, loaded with medical supplies and containers of food. 'Told Mum I was going out to do some night photography, experimenting with time exposure,' she grinned.

Having watched and learnt alongside her mother all her life, Addie expertly cleaned and dressed Piper's leg wound, securing a covering against infection.

While the patient tucked into the sandwiches and drank hot tea from the thermos lid, Addie asked, 'How's your family doing?'

'Mother's still as bossy,' she smiled fondly. 'A community elder now.'

'Ella was always a strong personality.'

Piper shrugged. 'Having a weird mother builds character. She and Jimmy still live out in the rented cottage on Jack's farm.'

The local butcher who ran cattle on the property. 'Does your Dad still work for him out there?'

'Yeah.'

'I see Kirra and Yarran around town when I'm home.' Addie mentioned Piper's sister and brother.

'Yeah. They've both got good jobs.'

Addie hesitated but decided to ask, 'So what have you been doing since you left school?'

'Bummed around for a while. Kinda lost, you

know? Then pulled myself together and did an arts diploma for two years.'

'You were always drawing something. Had a natural artist's eye. I loved your Aboriginal paintings best.'

'Yeah. Grandma taught me. I travel a lot and sell my stuff online.'

Addie decided to mention her concern about Piper's vulnerability out here and what she had in mind. 'Apart from the guys who have been trespassing, as I said this property is on the market so there might be people about. Real estate agent and buyers looking around. If you want to stay out of sight, probably not a good idea to stick around so I have a suggestion.'

Addie waited a moment to let Piper process that information and watched her guarded stare. 'So unless you plan on hobbling back to your vehicle and camping out in it, I can set you up in at the hollow camp down by the creek on our farm. I'll tell the family a friend needs some time alone. I go there myself sometimes so they know to keep out of the way. They'll respect your privacy. This time of year there's no cropping or harvesting so the men won't be about and needing to go into that creek paddock anyway.'

Piper seemed half receptive so Addie pressed on. 'Think about it and if you agree, text me. I'll set up the camp and return for you in the morning. Now, about your car. If you tell me where it is, I'll get my brother Nick to go check out the damage and fix it.' She chuckled. 'Don't look so alarmed. He's a top mechanic. He'll keep your secret.'

'At this rate,' she muttered, 'my location won't be private for long.' Judging by Piper's frown she was not at all convinced but grudgingly said, 'It's on the track leading into the nature reserve off Old Creek Road.'

'I know it.'

'It was the only place close with enough shelter to hide a car.'

'Right. I've brought a sleeping bag. It's on the motorbike. I'll go fetch it. You're not going to have a very comfortable night.'

Piper seemed unconcerned. 'I've slept rough before.'

Addie didn't doubt it.

'Thanks for all your help.' Piper sent Addie a strange meaningful glance. 'Sometimes meetings in life, like both of us being here at the homestead at the same time, can't be explained. More than coincidence. Almost magical.'

'I agree. However it happened or for whatever reason. I'm glad I was around when needed.'

When she returned home, Addie managed to catch Nick outside checking the dogs at their kennels for the night. She explained her friend's situation, but not her identity, without too many awkward questions from her brother. He agreed to go with Addie the following morning before he opened the garage in town.

So, immediately after breakfast next day, they drove separately to the location Piper had indicated.

When they found her vehicle and while Nick checked it over, Addie leant against the bonnet. 'Thanks for doing this. My friend's in a bit of a bind at the moment and can't afford much. I'll cover any costs.'

Nick had been on the ground inspecting the car underneath. As he emerged and stood again, he said wryly, 'It's okay, sis. It's an oldie for sure but reliable enough. Only needs some minor panel beating and the right front tyre replaced. I'll head into town for a new one and open the garage. My apprentice can hold the fort till I'm done here.'

'Thanks. Text me when it's ready?'

He nodded. Just then, Addie's mobile pinged

with a message from Piper. 'That's her now. I'm going to set her up at the creek camp for a day or so. Give her a chance to rest before she moves on.'

As Nick drove back into town, Addie returned to the farm, gathered her camping gear and headed in the ute across the paddock and back roads to the homestead. Piper had dragged a hay bale outside the tool shed and was sitting on it, making use of the weak sun.

'Morning. Sleep okay?'

'Fine.'

With a hand at Piper's elbow, Addie helped her into the farm ute, noticing she only had a small satchel. She was sure travelling light. Maybe she had more belongings in her car.

As they sped along the gravel road to the creek paddock, she said, 'Once I've set up camp for you, I'll get a fire going. I've brought eggs and bacon, and a thermos of Mum's soup. Should keep you going today.'

'Thanks,' Piper murmured, looking away out the side window.

Addie longed to probe but knew better. Piper had always been fiercely private and independent, and still seemed as mysterious and secretive as ever. By the time the tent was up and a fire going, Nick messaged that Piper's car was finished and he'd topped up the fuel tank.

When Addie relayed the information, her friend said, 'That's really generous. I should only need to stay tonight. My leg's not as bad today so

I should be fine to drive tomorrow,' she apologised.

'No hurry. Stay as long as you need. I'll call back later. You'll be private out here.' Addie gazed around. 'It's one of my favourite spots on the farm.'

As she drove away, she glanced in the rear mirror at the lonely sight of Piper sitting by the fire. Whatever reason had been the cause of threats and forced her here, she only hoped it was soon favourably resolved. For something was clearly not right in Piper Thorne's world.

Because she had been busy and preoccupied since Harry left the night before, Addie pulled up in the ute before leaving the paddock, wondering if she should keep him informed of the latest development about the homestead break in. Now the hacking dilemma was more or less sorted and on its path to being handled, did it even matter about the Banyandah connection?

Would Harry be interested that the burglars had returned? He was probably back in the city by now, having arranged to meet his father and reveal the Chandler Digital company peril. And, really, was there anything Harry could do anyway?

She tussled with a decision, only because Harry had made it clear he wanted them to pursue the Carlton Ross predicament together. She remembered his dark eyes deep with concern and his warning to be careful after she told him about the first time she had stumbled onto the two guys trespassing at the homestead.

He would be furious if she told him about last night and actually following the men into the house. Was it worth it? She might, just to stir him up. Ruffle that smooth city image. All the same, it was heartening to know he cared enough to be worried.

Plus he *had* also said he wanted to be involved every step of the way in this whole crisis and they *had* both agreed Banyandah and the current Ross family situation were somehow all tied up together.

Still unsure about anything where Harry Chandler was concerned, she was about to find out. Addie stepped from the ute, dropped the tailgate and sat on it swinging her legs with a view across the stubble paddock. She held her breath as his phone rang.

'Addie!'

His enthusiasm – or was it simply saying her name? – took her by surprise. 'Not interrupting you?'

'Never. Just had a breakfast meeting with the old man.'

'How did it go?'

'Wise move telling him after we obtained the evidence. If he was still living on the farm up here and Ross was his neighbour, I wouldn't doubt he'd have unlocked his rifle from the gun cabinet and marched over to confront him.' Amused respect filled Harry's voice. 'Plenty of fight left in my father yet. He was astonished to learn that uncovering the hacking crime and finding proof was all down to you.' Harry paused, then continued warmly, 'We're both deeply grateful, Addie.'

She had to wonder if she would ever hear it from Austin Chandler's own lips. And the irony didn't pass notice either. In the past, through prejudice, he had wrongfully refused her a job. Now, the woman he had overlooked as inadequate had just helped save his son's company.

'It was thanks to James in the end really.'

'Don't sell yourself short. You went above and beyond.'

'Just relieved we eventually achieved our goal.' She decided to raise the reason for her call. 'By the way, the suspicious activity around the homestead is ongoing.' She waited for his response to that teaser.

'What's happened?' Genuine interest there. Addie was pleased she had phoned him after all.

'Something and nothing. Yet. The two men returned last night after you left.'

'And you know this because?'

Oh dear, here it comes. 'I thought I saw flashing lights so I went over to investigate.'

'Naturally alone.' It wasn't a question. 'And?'

She omitted any mention of Piper, of course, but explained last night's homestead break in and the events that followed in the least alarming way possible. It didn't matter.

As expected, Harry still exploded. 'You followed them into the house! Addie, what were you thinking?'

She rolled her eyes toward the blue morning sky and focused on the underlying anxiety in his voice rather than his disapproval. 'To get evidence. There was no time to phone for help. They would have been gone by then. I needed to see if I could find out exactly why they were there and what they were after.' She justified her risk by outlining the details and implications of what she overheard. 'Obviously they've been hired to retrieve something from the cellar. Haven't the foggiest what it could possibly be; the place has been shut up for years. So you know what I think?'

'Do tell.' His harsh tone of a moment ago had moderated to tolerant amusement.

'I need to stake out the homestead and when they come back to get into the cellar, contact the police.'

'Wrong way round. You should warn Ewan first.'

Ah, the voice of reason. Addie heaved a lengthy sigh. 'Honestly, you're no fun. What if it's something small and silly, and we've wasted their time?'

'Didn't sound like it according to what you related of their conversation. It's more important than that. They're being paid for the job and doing it secretly. Can't possibly be legal. When they show up again, which sounds likely, it will be on a definite mission so at the least they need to be investigated if not stopped. Preferably caught in the act.'

'So I should tell Ewan?' Addie checked, unimpressed.

She had rather enjoyed the homestead adventure so far but, annoyingly, Harry was logical and right. It may be something or nothing but one thing was sure; a more crucial crime was about to take place. It was time to involve the law. She had already overstepped the mark last night but at least she now had definite information of a further plan when she phoned Ewan.

'The blokes won't be back till tonight,' Addie said reluctantly, 'but I'll call him now.'

'Don't sound so deprived,' he drawled.

'The burglars weren't carrying any weapons last night. Won't it alert them if police are crawling all over the place?'

'They'll keep a low profile. They've already broken the law by trespass and breaking in. Presuming they're caught for theft and depending on what they take, it'll be more than community service. Probably a fine or even gaol. Phone Ewan and I'll see you later.'

Addie almost fell off the tailgate. What? 'Aren't you in Melbourne?'

'I've already spoken to my father and I need

to call into the office but I'll be back late this afternoon.'

'You can spare the time?'

'I might have an idea.'

Sounded like a snap decision but although she dug, he refused to elaborate. Addie hung up, annoyed to be left ignorant, but intrigued. Harry always planned. His life was so structured and businesslike. But it would be a bonus to see him again. Which was getting to be a habit lately. Logical recently, of course, needing to work together but returning again so soon, wasn't that more like a choice?

Before she returned to the house, Addie made her final call to Ewan at the police station. Grateful for the information but she endured yet another reprimand about reporting it next time instead of investigating herself.

What was it with men these days?

In any event, Ewan sounded highly interested, mentioned that a patrol car would head out there and keep the homestead under surveillance with backup on alert if needed. He ended by suggesting she keep her distance from the property and leave it for the law to deal with now.

How utterly boring.

Addie spent the rest of the day helping her mother in the kitchen, putting together the makings of a barbeque for Piper tonight over at the creek camp and delivering it in person before sundown.

Piper looked brighter and walked easier than this morning.

'I'll leave tomorrow.' She glanced around. 'You're right about this place. It's like therapy. I'll pack up the tent first thing and douse the campfire.'

'No need but that would be helpful. I'd stay longer with you but I'm expecting a visitor. Text me when you're ready.'

'Thanks, Addie. I won't forget what you've done.'

'You're welcome.'

Unable to resist a bit more snooping, Addie drove the ute across the east paddock to the tree plantation along the fence line which gave her cover to spy on the homestead through the trees.

If you weren't looking for them, you wouldn't know they were there. Two patrol cars were well hidden in the shelter of bulloak scrub a distance from the homestead. As she watched, at least three officers were positioned and at vantage points closer in.

No doubt the foot patrol would move in first but, based on their previous night visits, the burglars chose late evening to haunt the place so the police might have a long wait.

While she longed to stay and watch events unfold, it wasn't quite dark yet. Assuming tonight was marked for the burglary, Addie decided to nick back to the farmhouse. See if

Harry had arrived, hear his idea then grab some food and return to watch the action.

How she would manage that without his interference she hadn't worked out. One thing was sure. He wasn't stopping her or taking away the pleasure in seeing the upshot of all this criminal subterfuge.

Chapter 10

As Addie drove up to the farmhouse, Harry's four wheel drive was already parked. Her whole mood lifted but her parents must be wondering why he was such a regular visitor recently after being a stranger for years with his life based in the city now.

They needn't get excited. It was for a reason, not any dormant interest in their single daughter.

Harry Chandler was a cool enigma all of his own. Addie had never really fully worked him out because he didn't readily give away much of himself. Although, to be honest, he *had* disclosed snippets lately since working together. She just admired the whole package. An honourable human being. A gentleman.

Raised with the same country values and respect for women as the Kendalls had instilled into their own sons while supporting and encouraging their only tomboy daughter to be true to herself and independent, advice she valued and followed. Even when it wasn't particularly cool for a girl to be a mathematical and IT nerd, she had forged her own path.

Done reflecting on Harry, Addie strode for the house, interested to hear his idea and scoot back to Banyandah. Be a pity to miss the action tonight no matter how long she had to wait.

She entered the cosy bustling kitchen to see Harry setting the table. Her heart sank. She didn't intend staying for dinner. Her mother wouldn't mind but how to abandon Harry without being rude if he tried to talk her out of her homestead vigil. Not that she would listen but that meant avoiding a disagreement in front of the folks. She could just see her stimulating evening disappearing. There was no one she would rather see than Harry Chandler. Just not right now.

'Here she is.' Her mother beamed. 'You've been a dark horse.'

Addie panicked for a moment, hoping Piper hadn't been disturbed or approached. She had given her word on privacy.

'Harry's just been telling us about the homestead.'

Addie's relief was epic. 'Oh, yes. A bit exciting.'

She only hoped he hadn't mentioned her dubious night excursion alone into the depths of a deserted old house with a pair or dodgy burglars.

Harry moved forward behind her mother, raised his eyebrows and winked. 'I was just telling Julie about my idea.'

Addie had no clue what was happening but it sounded like she was meant to play along. 'You did?'

'Better that we go together this time, don't you think?'

She would go anywhere with Harry but was intrigued about what she was agreeing to. 'Of course.'

'So I've already mentioned we'll skip dinner and head straight over to the homestead in case Ewan needs any further input from you.' His dark eyed gaze was actually pleading.

Really? His idea was the same as hers? To spy on the police stakeout? And *he* was begging *her* to agree? Some turnaround.

She rather hoped it wasn't just to keep an eye on her, although she supposed that was flattering. But to come all this way from Melbourne to do it? She would need to play down the kick of butterflies in her stomach at the thought of spending time alone in the dark with Harry. Not give away her joy at the amazing turn of events tonight. One moment believing her plan would be ruined, the next she was apparently sharing it with the man of her dreams.

Stunned, Addie's mind blanked. Who was this new flexible and surprising Harry Chandler? Ditching his city responsibilities for a night watch with a childhood friend in the bush? She noticed her mother had already boiled the kettle to fill a thermos which was placed alongside a container of food.

'Just some warm sausage rolls and savoury toasties. Nice of Harry to let me know in advance.'

He'd phoned ahead? 'Very thoughtful.'

Addie privately grinned. Like her daughter, Julie Kendall had been charmed. Especially since her initial indignation when Harry had suddenly reappeared in all their lives after the Chandler slight to her daughter of years ago. Time, new perceptions and informed respect had now replaced the family's former caution.

In no time, Addie had shrugged on her parka and beanie against the autumn night chill. 'Thanks, Mum.' She kissed her then marched outside ahead of Harry, gallantly carrying their supplies, before he changed his mind. 'Leave your shiny vehicle here. We'll take the paddock basher.'

'Whatever you say.'

'So amenable tonight,' Addie teased. 'You told a few porkies back there.'

'Not really. All in a good cause.'

Leaving the farmhouse, Addie felt like she and Harry were two truant kids escaping school. Hardly, but the mood was the same. Incredibly, he seemed to have a mutual sense of expectation about tonight's escapade.

They climbed into the ute, Addie finding it bizarre and unexpected to have a jeans and windcheater-clad Harry sitting alongside in their old unregistered family faithful, complete with crunchy gears and the odd spot of rust. He seemed unphased and totally at home because he had grown up around here, even it if was further south in pastoral country.

Addie had trouble connecting the school age boy of her memories with today's grown man.

'I've already found the perfect spot,' she said as they bumped across the paddock.

'Cheeky.' She noticed he grabbed the handrail above the door.

'I thought you of all people would appreciate my forward planning.'

'I do. I'm impressed.'

'This idea is so out of character for you. Why did you *really* suggest it?'

He paused then said quietly, 'It seemed important to you.'

Addie was rarely lost for words but how to respond to that? So she didn't, at least not immediately. 'So it wasn't because you were against me being on my own around crims?'

He chuckled. 'I could have asked one of your brothers instead.'

Indeed he could. So why hadn't he? 'But you came yourself. Bit rash, even for you. No matter who tagged along, I was going anyway you know.'

'Of course you were. And I admit to having a sneaky fascination for knowing any secret the homestead is hiding as much as you.'

Once they reached the tree plantation, Addie cut the headlights and parked the ute. Loaded with their night picnic, they tramped by torchlight to within looming sight of the rear of the house and settled down, huddled close against the cold, bodies touching, backed up against the trunk of a gum tree.

Knowing how sounds carried across open flat country on a still night, in between munching on sausage rolls, Addie said in a low voice, 'I'll feel a right twit if the men don't appear soon. Or at all.'

'We wouldn't be here if we didn't expect them. Ewan has rightly taken this seriously.'

'I guess the burglars *have* been predictable.'

As time ticked by, with every minute dragged out and feeling longer, Harry was quiet, until, 'I've been wracking my brain trying to work out what anyone could possibly need to recover so suddenly from this house that has lain empty for years. And if it was so important, why have they never done it before?'

'Top question. Fingers crossed we find out soon.'

More time lingered with agonising inactivity. They had eaten all the food and were sipping on mugs of hot tea.

Addie sensed Harry's restless unease beside her so it was hardly a surprise when he said, 'We shouldn't waste our waiting time.'

She wondered not only how, but why he expected or needed to fill the peacefulness and mystery on this crisp autumn night.

'People aren't meant to be cramming every

second of their day. Nothing wrong with a little quiet time.' Turning aside to glance at him, it was clear from his frown she had dented his idea without at least hearing it. 'What are you thinking then? Twenty questions?' she quipped.

He shrugged. 'Me first then.'

'That's cheating. You haven't told me your idea.'

'You didn't give me a chance. So, now I know the truth about James,' he said wryly, 'I'm surprised you don't have a boyfriend or partner in your life.'

'How do you know I don't?'

'He'd be around.'

'Maybe he lives in the city.' She half-turned toward him and caught the edge of his mouth tilt into a grin.

'Unlikely,' he drawled.

Then why was she so attracted to this urban eyeful? She resisted answering because her romantic life was pathetic.

'No one in your past?' he persisted.

'A few made an impression.' And he hadn't a clue he was included in that number. The others were barely considered at the time which she would never admit because her heart lay elsewhere. So she fired back at him, 'You claimed you've been too busy for a woman in your life. Is that really true?'

He chewed over her question for a moment before responding. 'I guess I've had acquaintances more than relationships. A female on my arm for a social function. A duty date. That sort of thing.'

'How uninspiring and practical.' Where was the romance? 'No serious contenders for your heart?'

'That would be telling.'

'You must have met some stunning women over the years.' It hurt to even mention it.

Harry heaved a sigh. Of regret? Fond memory? 'Sure, and that was probably my mistake. I went for a slinky body, bedroom hair and long legs.'

Addie was jolted by his blunt honesty, hardly expecting him to be a monk yet rather relieved he didn't have anyone special hiding in the wings. Then again, perhaps he did and was simply being tactful.

'That's why I was never in the running,' she laughed to cover her disappointment in not being his type.

'Shorter is cute. And you've always had bedroom hair.'

Addie's heart skipped a beat at the suggestion even as her mind grew confused by his sudden switch of interest. Still flustered, she shrugged and said easily, 'Mum always preferred me to leave it long. As an adult, I guess I've never bothered to chop it off.'

'Don't ever do that. Your hair is gorgeous.'

'How would you know? I always tie it back.'

There was a pause and a long steady look of challenge. 'Let it down.'

Addie was shocked but thrilled with surprise at the twist in their conversation and Harry's suddenly seductive mood toward her. 'Really?' He nodded. 'Now?'

'Please,' he murmured, running the back of his hand down her arm before reaching over and raising it to slowly remove her beanie, revealing her braided ponytail.

Addie's heart raced as she brought her long plait over her shoulder, untied the band, untangled its length and combed her fingers through the resulting waves to spread them out.

Harry was already sitting close but turned to face her, stroking a hand from the top of her head down the flow of hair rustling across her shoulders and back. When his hand settled against her nape and his fingers threaded through the strands, a captivated Addie drowned in his gaze. All the expressions on his face and in his eyes told her exactly what she wanted to know. Harry Chandler was making a move on Addie Kendall.

'I'm not a toy, Chandler. Don't play with me.'

'Promise,' he whispered as his head dipped closer.

She hoped this wasn't just filling in time on a cold dark night. Taking advantage. Knowing the man better these days, she trusted his word, knowing he was above shallow moves, and leant into him. She had waited a long time for this and when their warm lips met, she wasn't disappointed.

Soft and searching and genuine. He was equally putting true feelings behind the intimate moment. He lingered, kissed her more and longer. Drew her tight against him, heartbreaking tenderness in every touch.

With an arm around her shoulder, she sank into his warmth, her head nestling into the curve of his neck, his chin resting on the top of her waterfall of hair. She yawned with weary relaxation.

'It's well after ten,' he murmured.

'Hope the police think this stakeout is worthwhile.'

'Somehow I believe it will be. In every respect.' His words held double meaning.

As Addie closed her eyes, soaking in the afterglow of affection, she wondered if life would be awkward with Harry later. Or would he take the lead and follow up this breakthrough moment. Offer to phone, suggest a date. At the least, keep in touch. Her thoughts drifted between concern and pleasure.

She must have dozed because Harry was gently nudging her. She opened her eyes and mumbled, 'What time is it?'

'Almost eleven.' His voice was loaded with excitement. 'Lights.'

Addie sat up and scrambled to her feet.

Harry stood, too. The van was back. The headlights threw the action into clear view. No police stirred as the two familiar men emerged from the vehicle and slid open its side door, dragging out bags and tools. Their purpose tonight was intense, moving to the back door, heaving it open and immediately disappearing inside.

Within moments, the dark shapes of police officers spread out and converged with organised stealth on the homestead, some remaining stationed outdoors, others stalking the burglars into the house. And it looked like Ewan was leading that team.

Tense moments passed with no sounds or action.

'Damn nuisance not knowing what's happening,' Addie complained, slipping her cold hands into her pockets.

'Patience,' Harry whispered, pulling her close.

The ten minutes they waited felt like ten hours. Seconds crawled.

'What's the holdup?' Addie grew restless.

'They'll want to wait and catch the guys with the goods.'

Then the evening's stillness suddenly exploded with the noise of voices, yelling and scuffling. As though the police were demanding instructions or their offenders resisting arrest. Somewhere in the dark, police radios crackled into life and more men outside went into the house.

A while later, Ewan and three of his men emerged with both burglars handcuffed and marched them across to their vehicles. Ewan barked out instructions then spoke urgently and at length on his phone. With no longer any need for secrecy, lights went on everywhere, flooding the scene.

'Seems like a lot of action for a simple burglary arrest,' Addie said. 'I wonder what they found?'

'We'll find out eventually.'

Addie edged forward away from the shelter of the trees.

'What are you doing?' Harry challenged.

'The guys are in custody. Ewan won't mind.'

'Addie-'

'I gave him the information.' She heard a gasp of frustration from Harry.

Behind her, he caught up. 'At least take it slow and keep your distance.'

Addie respected the police operation enough to hang back but well within range of Ewan's notice. Eventually he caught sight of her but did not look pleased and strode to meet them.

'You shouldn't be here,' he ordered. 'This is a crime scene.'

'You got them. What did you find?'

Addie noticed he turned into media mode and carefully chose his words. 'More than we bargained for. The men both claim they had no idea what they were hired to recover.' He paused. 'Not a word, understand?' Addie nodded. 'This is more than trespass and theft. I've called for backup. It's a potential crime scene now.' Ewan flashed a glance between his stunned listeners. 'We may be dealing with a possible homicide here.'

With both Addie and Harry speechless at the admission, Ewan urged, 'You guys need to leave. We'll be taping off the entire homestead block so forensics can get to work when they arrive. Addie, come into the station in the morning. We may need more details from you. Confirm what you've already told us. See if there's anything further you can add.'

'Sure.' With packing up Piper at the creek camp first thing, she said, 'Late morning? Elevenish?'

Ewan nodded. 'Appreciate the tip off but you both need to scoot. Let the guys get on with the job. We may know more tomorrow.'

As they turned and walked away, Addie exchanged a horrified glance with Harry who quietly reached for her hand. She found the small gesture comforting in the light of Ewan's statement.

'Someone was in there?' she whispered.

A body. In Banyandah. In the cellar.

'Are you thinking what I'm thinking?'

Harry shrugged. 'Probably.'

'Hudson Ross,' they said together.

By torchlight, they collected their picnic remains and returned to the ute.

'This will be nothing shy of the district shockwave of the century,' Addie said as they grappled with the significance of the discovery.

It also occurred to her how timely that she had moved Piper only hours before all this happened. With police swarming all over the place, her friend may have become a person of interest, if not a prime suspect.

'What a mess for Morgan Ross,' Harry said in the ute on the way back to the farm.

'Can you imagine his reaction when he's notified what they found tonight on his property? All hell will break loose.' Addie frowned in reflection. 'You have to wonder who the last person was to shut and padlock the cellar door.'

'The culprit.'

That fact slumped them into silence.

Since it was already after midnight, when they reached the farmhouse it was in darkness.

'I guess the folks will hear about the local news tomorrow,' Addie said as she stepped out.

Harry already had their picnic gear in hand and sauntered beside her to the back door. He set down the empty thermos and container, and sank his hands into his pockets. 'Okay if I swing by tomorrow?'

Knowing she was helping Piper leave in the morning and had an appointment at the police station, Addie tussled with when exactly that could be.

Seeing her hesitation, Harry said, 'I meant everything between us tonight.'

'I hope so.' Didn't hurt to let him know she was being cautious.

'I'd like to keep in touch. See more of you.'

She would like nothing more but grinned. 'Good luck with managing that. I'm a country woman again, remember?'

After a long line of leggy model types, she wondered if Harry's interest might fade. If he really cared for her long enough to stick around then he would prove it with actions not words. After a lifetime of adoration for this man, she was sure of her feelings. But after only weeks of reconnection, was he?

'We'll work something out.'

The confident way he said it sounded like he already had ideas. They were on the same page about tonight's homestead stakeout so she was interested to know what he had in mind. The possibility of figuring out the distance dilemma between them gave her a glimmer of hope.

And when he brushed aside a lock of wavy hair to tuck it behind her ear before bending for more serious kissing again, she was prepared to give him the benefit of the doubt about pretty much anything. For now.

He kissed her nose, murmured, 'Night,' and left, Addie's body humming with waves of physical need for the guy. She had best keep her emotions locked up and under control until this crazy new buzz with Harry worked itself out.

All the same, later in the early hours she found it tricky being pleasantly tired yet unable to sleep, remembering the amazing moments tonight so intimately nestled with Harry in the dark. Their murmured conversation and the satisfaction to wake after dozing to find she had comfortably nodded off for a while, her head resting against his shoulder.

She could only hope this new magnetism drawing them closer would become more than fantasy.

Chapter 11

Next morning, despite a lack of sleep, Addie woke with the late autumn sunrise and padded out to the kitchen in her trackie pyjamas where Julie was already bustling with breakfast for the men.

'Didn't hear you come in last night, dear.'

'It was late. Didn't want to wake you.'

While the family was all gathered around before dispersing in different directions for the day, Addie took the opportunity to break the startling news of the body found in the homestead cellar. For once, her brothers actually paid attention and gaped. Speechless in amazement at the Banyandah bombshell.

'That place has been closed up for years,' Darren said from his seat at the table.

Her mother added, 'Suppose it's been in there all this time.'

Judging by the frowns and raised eyebrows, everyone clearly had their own private thoughts on the unfortunate person's identity but incredibly no one actually voiced them. However the coincidence was too eerie to ignore. The new disclosure and the likelihood sank the family into silence.

Once the news broke in the community, it would be the only topic of conversation and spread like a summer bushfire around the district. With far reaching consequences. If the Ross family were about to be publicly exposed and shamed over their IT company violation, when the truth came to light behind the body discovery, it would mean even further uncomfortable embarrassment and sticky scandal.

Personally affected by the IT humiliation and fallout, Addie held her own suspicions about the two recent random events happening so close together. Far too coincidental involving the same family not to be connected even though one had taken place in the city and the latest one in the bush.

To think she had worked for Morgan Ross and sat in his office across that massive desk, facing the tyrant, being arrogantly belittled. The impact of the outcome was finally beginning to sink into her head space and emotions. And not in the best way.

Addie filled a bowl of porridge and sat on the lounge to eat it, feet tucked beneath her. Mitch walked past and playfully flicked the ends of her tousled wavy hair. 'Don't usually see you with your hair down, sis.'

She flushed and murmured, 'I'm not awake yet.'

'You actually look like a girl for a change,' he

teased, accepting a plate of cooked breakfast from his mother and taking it to join his father at the table.

Although Addie was long accustomed to her brothers' ribbing, she felt a twinge of regret and discomfort. Since childhood she had dressed for country life and continued the habit to university and the workplace. Had she allowed the familiar style to become too comfortable?

Her thoughts flew to Harry and last night. How feminine he had made her feel even before he asked her to leave her hair down. Staring into the open fire reflecting, she became aware of a disruption to the mood in the room.

'Harry,' her mother said, 'you won't have had much sleep. Up till all hours and back again already.'

Addie felt like disappearing into the sofa. Who visits even before people are dressed? Then she realised she was the only odd one out and burned with embarrassment.

'Morning, Addie,' he said from across the room, his lazy drawl loaded with humour.

'Harry.' She braved a glance in his direction. Already dressed and looking fresh and handsome.

When Julie offered him breakfast, he shook his head. 'Already eaten, thanks.'

'Not just a scrap of toast or muesli I hope.' She indicated Mitch's half empty plate. 'Sure you wouldn't like one of those?'

'Tempting.' As her mother smiled at him and raised her shoulders in question, Harry laughed. 'Mrs. Kendall you're a hard woman to resist.'

'Done.'

Within seconds she produced a huge plate of scrambled eggs, bacon and tomatoes and set it before him with a decent slab of toasted homemade bread.

Addie didn't understand why that simple exchange between Harry and her mother should leave her feeling so satisfied. She muttered something about a shower, rose and escaped.

When she returned fifteen minutes later, her brothers were gone and she had noticed her father in the farm office as she passed, leaving only Harry and her mother in the kitchen.

His gaze roamed over her with interest. Perhaps he was staring because she hadn't confined her hair in its usual plait. Just tied it back in a great bunch of wavy ripples. It had seemed quicker at the time but she now realised Harry may well believe she had done it for him.

With his hands wrapped around a mug of tea, he said, 'You're cute first thing in the morning.'

OMG. In front of her mother? He was as bad as her brothers. Julie turned away but failed to hide her surprised grin at this flirty exchange. Addie could have whacked Harry with her boot if it wasn't already on her foot.

'If you mean the PJs, very funny.'

She covered her terror with responding humour that he should so openly express his interest - after all these years – before she was more certain of his motives. He had only kissed her for the first time ever last night. Why the rush? She was no innocent. There had been one or two steamy, if brief, relationships in her life. Besides, he was making it impossible and awkward to leave when she had a commitment to Piper.

She hadn't seen Harry for years. Now he was around every day. That should thrill her, right? Instead, she grew anxious by what she couldn't deny seemed like his genuine attention. Except now she had it, what could possibly come of it? City and country probably wouldn't work. So far this Harry thing was flimsy and wonderful. Fragile. He was the only man who could break her heart because it had always been his.

Thankfully, Julie made herself scarce with an excuse about feeding the chooks. Leaving her alone with Harry. Baffled why he was here.

He rose and rinsed his mug in the sink. 'Going into town to the police station?'

'Later. I have an errand I need to do first.'

'Can I tag along?'

Could this get worse? She would offend him. 'Sorry. It's a personal thing with a girlfriend.'

He frowned, clearly feeling rejected but suggested, 'Maybe we could catch up for lunch?'

'I can't promise. Not sure how long it will

take at the station with Ewan and when I'll be free.'

She hated turning him down and giving the impression she wasn't interested. And because Piper had already sent a text this morning, she had an overriding urge to get back to the creekside camp. As much as the homestead saga loomed large in their lives at the moment, she still needed to help her friend.

Harry's gaze told her he was unconvinced with her excuses. 'Are you okay?'

'Yes. Fine.'

'The hacking is resolved and my legal process is underway. There's nothing more either of us can do on that front. And we all have to wait for any further developments on the body found in the homestead.'

'I know that,' Addie said irritably, wishing she could confide the other problem on her mind.

Then he would know her reason was genuine and she wasn't trying to fob him off or keep him at a distance. Because, without realising it these past weeks, Harry had become her support and strength, the one person outside family she appreciated having by her side in her personal troubles.

'Sure there's not something bothering you?' he persisted.

'No, why do you ask?' Harry was beginning to understand her too well which tended to come with familiarity. Plenty of that around between them lately.

'You seem distracted today.'

'Do I? Guess I am a bit. Lots to do.'

Addie hated having to conceal anything from Harry but she was not at liberty to disclose anything of Piper's plight.

He moved toward the door leading out to the back porch. 'I'll leave you to it. Actually,' he hesitated, 'the body found last night and its identity and consequences may have implications for my legal case. We'll keep a lid on our pending law suit. Don't need to make the situation worse for Carlton Ross right now. We're only seeking justice for the IT theft.'

'Fair enough. Once your legal case is proved, I'll launch my own personal claim for wrongful dismissal and appropriate compensation. It's not about any money.' Addie felt compelled to justify her reason.

'I know that.'

'I need an admission of wrongdoing and an apology.'

'We'll work everything out.' He paused. 'I'm expected in Melbourne for consultations with my lawyers this afternoon. The case needs all my attention now so I might be down there for a while.'

He had wanted to see her before he left. That meant something, didn't it? She felt like the worst friend, virtually pushing him away and he had keenly sensed that uncertainty.

'Will you be coming back?' Addie asked too quickly and immediately despised herself for it.

Harry eyed her from beneath a furrowed brow. 'Going to miss me?' he teased.

No way would Addie admit her childhood feelings hadn't disappeared. In fact, since being back in Harry's life, she was shocked how swiftly and how much, with the slightest encouragement, they had burst into new life. How could they not when he kissed with such tenderness and passion?

'Get over yourself, Chandler,' she said softly. 'You're not irresistible.'

Totally a lie and exactly the right thing to say if she wanted to drive the man from her life again. Addie grew desolate at the thought, her heart pathetically miserable every time he left.

So when Harry's beautiful mouth pulled into a tight line and his dark gaze raked her from her head of mostly untamed hair to the toes of her boots, it was like he was committing her to memory. Which made her grow hot with longing. But he didn't reach out for her, make any attempt to touch. He didn't lean closer for a kiss in that already familiar way making her heart and mind misbehave with very earthy thoughts and desires.

Her returning pleading gaze sent out a challenge. *Want me. Miss me. What you started could be the beginning of a beautiful relationship.*

Damn it. The flirting eyes were all for

nothing. He was walking away. No goodbye, no kiss, no promises. Her heart broke right down the middle when the diesel motor rumbled into life and its tyres crunched on the gravelled driveway. He didn't wave or look back.

She already knew fairy tales didn't always come true. A girl didn't always get the guy at the end of a book. But Harry Chandler was no longer a country boy and she was a country girl. Feeling miserable and forsaken, she knew now she loved him with all her heart. But more than her home town? More than the Wimmera? Would she leave this place and go anywhere with him? Heartsick and uncertain, that was a question it was impossible to answer right now.

As she was about to head indoors, Julie returned from the chook yard with a basin of eggs. 'Harry gone?'

'Yes, back to the city.'

'Well now, you have your own future to consider, don't you dear?' she said kindly, understanding as mothers do what feelings were at play here, trying to soften the blow.

'Not right this moment, Mum.'

Addie had never let the grass grow under her feet. Keeping busy was the coping strategy she had always used in the past. Missing Harry since the moment he drove away, and terrified to admit it even to herself, she hoped it worked this time, too.

First up, Piper was waiting. On her way to the creek camp in Gertie, because she couldn't drive the unregistered farm ute on public roads, Addie couldn't resist taking the long way around.

She swung by the homestead, cruising slow as she passed. The property was taped off from the front gate with patrolling police everywhere. Already a few cars were parked at the roadside. Media perhaps.

Suddenly a young man who had been lounging against a generic white SUV pushed himself away from it and deliberately stepped out in front of her crawling vehicle, forcing her to brake. He moved around from the bonnet and tapped on her window.

The nerve of the drongo. Beyond weary from being falsely accused of something she did not do, losing her job, falling for a guy who may never be able to love her back and anxious over a friend who was clearly in trouble, Addie's patience was thin.

She manually wound down the window. 'What on earth do you think you're doing?' He was actually handsome in a rugged unshaven kind of way. And neatly dressed.

He ignored her question and jumped in with one of his own. 'What's going on here?'

'Are you a reporter?'

He didn't reply. Instead, he whipped out a photograph and rudely flashed it in her face. 'Have you seen this woman around?'

Whoa. Addie reeled back at the sight of Piper's face. This was too much of a coincidence. Was this person responsible for forcing her friend off the road?

She held up both hands and nodded toward the police barrier at the homestead gate. 'With all this happening? Anyone would be turned away.'

Undeterred, the man produced a business card and handed it to Addie. 'If you see or hear anything, this is how you can reach me.'

A private investigator. 'Is she in trouble?'

He shrugged. 'People are concerned. They'd like to find her. She may be in danger.'

Yeah, Addie thought wryly, but from who? Suspicion had kicked in the moment he appeared. She grabbed his card, stuffed it in her pocket and sped away.

As she bumped over the paddock track and approached the creek hollow, Piper was already waiting, the tent down and packed away, campfire doused.

Addie strode toward her and, although she didn't feel like it because she bore disturbing news, she smiled. 'Morning.'

As they heaved the camp gear into Gertie's boot, Piper was fascinated by Addie's old car. 'Great wheels.'

She was pleased to hear it. Not everyone appreciated classic cars. 'How are you feeling?'

'Better. I won't have any trouble driving.'

'We should get going and it might be an idea

to sink low in your seat.' Addie produced the stranger's business card, showed Piper and explained her encounter.

'Ben Powell.' She frowned. 'Name's not familiar.' Addie described his features and Piper shook her head. 'Doesn't sound like anyone I know.'

'He was driving a white SUV.'

Piper's mouth twisted. 'Could be the car that ran me off the road,' she offered vaguely. 'But it was dark and I was trying to keep my wheels on the road so I didn't have time for a good look at the vehicle or the driver.'

Then Addie related the tragic homestead news. 'So we definitely need to get you way from here. Now. Police are crawling all over the place.'

'Don't worry,' Piper assured her, 'I'm not wanted by police. Mine is a private family matter. But whoever that Ben guy is, I know who probably sent him.'

Addie grew alarmed. Piper's life was dangerous at the moment if Ben Powell had been hired to find her. 'I hope all this secrecy and being hunted is worth it.'

Strangely, Piper didn't answer.

They climbed into Gertie, Piper keeping low and wearing Addie's beanie over her short hair. They travelled the back way to the reserve where Piper's car was hidden, watching up and down every road for any other vehicles.

When Piper scrambled out and unlocked her

car, Addie produced a hamper of food and sat it on the back seat.

'Thanks for all you've done. I usually don't ask for help.'

'You have my mobile number. Use it any time.'

'I'll pay you back one day. Somehow,' she promised softly, looking back at Addie, her expression vulnerable and serious.

'No need. At some point, we all need to reach out to others.'

And wasn't that exactly what she had done both for, and to, Harry Chandler? With his help freely offered and given in return.

She hesitated before leaving, seeking to reassure her desperate friend. 'I hope everything turns out okay for you.'

'Thanks,' Piper whispered, managing a weak smile.

'Keep in touch.' Probably useless suggesting it but Addie felt deep concern for Piper's precarious situation.

'If I can.'

'Good luck.'

Addie gave her a quick hug, jumped back in Gertie and drove from the sheltered reserve, careful before emerging out onto the road that no other vehicles were in sight.

All she could do now was send out positive vibes and prayers that her childhood friend, Piper Thorne, stayed safe. But she couldn't stem a degree of intrigue and deeper concern, and would forever wonder about the root of her family problem.

Chapter 12

Addie sped into town for her interview with Ewan Holt. 'Manage any sleep?' she greeted him, noting the face stubble and edge of weariness even on such a powerful fit man.

'Not much,' he admitted, leading her into a private room. 'I'm on a break soon.'

She re-read and revised her original statement, adding further details, then signed it off.

Ewan seemed more relaxed and leaned back in his chair. 'I can't tell you much. Morgan Ross has been informed of the discovery in his homestead overnight. Naturally there would have been shock and the assumed possibility of some connection with the disappearance of his brother, Hudson.'

'We've all had thoughts along that line.'

'Because of that potential background history,' he continued, 'Morgan would have been questioned about who was last in the homestead, the cellar in particular. Any other family members who could possibly have visited since then. That kind of thing. Obviously it's most likely the body was left after the house was unoccupied.

'So, for now, forensics are processing the scene and collecting evidence about the cause of death. Unfortunately it will take time to identify the remains from DNA. If there's no family match, it will be even longer. Unless other information comes forward.'

The way Ewan hedged, Annie understood he knew more but couldn't say. 'What will happen to the burglars?'

'They're still being interviewed before providing statements. Actually, they're proving rather helpful now they know what they were paid to retrieve. Higher stakes loosens tongues.'

'So your investigation will take its course.'

'As always. Still plenty of questions without answers but we're gradually working through.' Ewan slowly rose. Her cue to leave. 'Thanks for coming in.'

Addie stood too. 'You're welcome. Didn't know when I reported a simple burglary what it would lead to.'

'We're grateful. When the body is eventually identified, a family will have answers and closure. But next time,' he drawled, opening the door for her, 'don't follow burglars into an isolated deserted house. Phone us first.'

Addie chuckled and before really thinking about it blurted out, 'Harry said the same thing.' As soon as the words left her mouth, she cringed.

'He's been seen around the Wimmera a lot lately.'

Annie shrugged it off. 'We've had business matters in common to deal with.'

'So you keep in touch?'

She certainly hoped so and crossed her fingers behind her back. 'We're old school friends.'

In the following week with Harry back in Melbourne finalising his legal case, Addie tackled her future. Alternately, she worked on her two new websites for an online IT consultancy business offering her services under short term contract, and an online business promoting and selling her photographic work.

When she needed a break from the computer, she moved all of her bedroom furniture into the middle of the room, climbed a ladder and began rolling paint onto the ceiling and walls. In between waiting for each coat to dry, she could be found helping in her mother's kitchen, doing chores around the farm, or speeding around paddocks on the motor bike. All of which made her realise how much she loved this life.

Other times she wandered out to the sheds where Nick was doing check-ups and maintenance on their big machinery with his farming brothers prior to cropping which would start soon following the first breaking autumn rains.

From time to time, the real estate agent phoned so she buzzed into town to view yet another potential new home but without enthusiasm for any of them. Addie wasn't usually a picky person but there always seemed to be something not quite right with each property. Mostly they lacked surrounding acres and gum trees so she began to consider the option of a farmlet. Maybe using part for herself and either subdividing the remainder or leasing and agistment for neighbours.

For no reason she could explain, Addie's heart wasn't fully invested in her search but she persisted.

With regular phone calls from Harry sounding busy and weary, it was a relief to receive contact from the Melbourne estate agent renting her old terrace. Finally it had been re-let so Addie needed to head for the city to pick up her few remaining belongings. She could have done it sooner but, life. So she refuelled Gertie at Nick's garage before she left town.

A big mug of strong hot tea was usually Addie's preference but on this chilly day, strangely, some random instinct caused her to stop at the Coach Roadhouse and indulge in a hot keep mug of coffee. Holly commented on the Banyandah homestead report in the media and all of its implications. The news had raged fast through the district and a local highway stop was certainly a hangout for spreading rumours, especially when it involved an unknown body.

From across the counter while she prepared

Addie's order, Holly said guardedly, 'Because of what they found, the police have contacted me about my missing mother. They already have my DNA from the original case so I just wait to see if it's a match.'

Addie's heart went out to her. 'This will be an anxious time for you.'

Holly sighed. 'Honestly, after all this time, I don't mind. I just need to know.'

'Of course.'

Once Addie continued her journey, she grew unsettled and troubled for both Piper Thorne and Holly Duncan, both with unresolved mysteries in their lives.

Back in Melbourne again, fortunately only briefly, Addie always felt a stubborn kick of proud spirit to be driving her faithful old Gertie. She was always a standout on the freeways alongside modern vehicles and followed her usual route, leaving the M1 and skirting the city fringes out to Fitzroy.

It was no longer bittersweet bundling up the last of her gear in the terrace because she knew in her heart she belonged in the Wimmera. A choice made despite the gaping discrepancy of Harry living in the city and the nagging difficult personal situation that created.

Thinking of Harry, Addie tapped out a quick text to him, crossed fingers he had even a small amount of time to meet on her whistle stop visit. She could be flexible with whatever he suggested.

She had most of today, would sleep one last time in the terrace tonight, hand in the keys to her estate agent in the morning and still leave most of tomorrow free for anything that fate cast her way. Especially with Harry but she also had other catch-ups in mind.

Not immediately getting a response from Harry, Addie texted Kimberley Ross. Who was fortunately free. Addie found a dress, pulled on her favourite denim jacket and wound a scarf around her neck. In concession to a city day and hopefully also seeing Harry, she tugged on low heeled dress boots, giving her a little extra height. For once she decided to leave her trusty farm pair aside. She sighed over her hair, eventually opting for the time saver of no braid and tying it back in a wild bunch. With a slash of pale lipstick and one final glance in a mirror, Addie figured she would do.

To save time because every moment counted on this short city trip, she grabbed a cab and met Kimberley in a cosy intimate café in Toorak village.

'Perfect choice,' Addie hugged her when they met.

'One of my favourites. I've booked a table. Come sit.'

While they sipped hot drinks awaiting their lunch orders, Addie hesitated to begin the conversation. It was tricky timing for the Ross family with the gruesome homestead discovery in recent days and no answers yet but she had a purpose to pursue and Kimberley was the ideal person to help achieve it. Perhaps this chat would prove a distraction.

As it happened, Kimberley anticipated her concerns. 'Elephant in the room first. The family is in upheaval on many fronts at the moment as you can imagine. Father demanded Logan and I attend the house and grilled us on a number of questions.' She frowned. 'Logan seemed evasive but that's nothing new. His mind is usually elsewhere. Our parents are bickering. Not a pretty sight. I guess we'll survive but it's not easy being hounded by the media. Any whiff of scandal and they're vultures.'

'I can't begin to imagine what you're going through.'

'Sucks. But what can you do? If you're high profile, you're a target.' Their meals arrived and as they tucked in, Kimberley added, 'Lovely to see you down here again by the way.'

'Just two days. Ending my terrace rental and wanted to see you. I had a chat to Stephanie when she started working for your father's company and I was interested to learn she has studied fashion design.'

'Steph has always sketched dresses. As kids she would watch all those old movies where the women wore lovely gowns and feminine clothes. She's a whizz with any material, a dummy model, a tin of pins, scissors and a sewing machine.'

'It sounded to me that she's putting Logan first and supporting his life ahead of her own. I was wondering if you had any ideas for encouraging her to take her talent seriously and start putting her designs out there in the fashion world. I was hoping you might know some contacts to try and make that happen.'

'Sure. I've nagged her before about that exact same thing. Her talent is natural and I'd love to be part of launching her on that path. She has made up one or two exclusive individual designs for me. I know Steph has a portfolio of her work. I'll invite her for lunch, you come too and we'll see if we can't convince her to get something rolling. Meanwhile I'll phone a few boutique owners I know personally so that I have some ammunition to put in front of her when we meet. Hopefully she'll ramp up her courage and put forward a proposal to them.' Kimberley grew excited and offered high praise for Addie's generosity. 'I just know with our encouragement she'll seriously take on board what we suggest.'

Finishing their coffees later, Kimberley said, 'By the way, Addie, just so you know. At school back in the Wimmera, I thought you were a gutsy kid. You were always fair and genuine but nobody mistreated you in the playground because you sure could take care of yourself.'

Addie laughed, not sure whether to be proud or offended. 'Was I that bad?'

'No,' Kimberley said quickly, 'you were that

good. In your own sure way, a role model even back then. Go you,' she ended warmly, 'and especially for wanting to help Steph.'

'Just paying it forward. She unknowingly helped me. Let me know when you can arrange a get-together with her.'

'Will do.' Kimberley checked her phone. 'I should get back to the gallery. Great to meet. Ciao.'

As Addie waited for a taxi to take her who-knew-where next, Harry finally phoned in response to her text.

'Hey you.'

Addie dissolved at the warmth and depth of intimacy in his voice. 'I'm in the city.'

He groaned. 'Great. Been thinking of you.'

'I know you're busy and this was a long shot but I'm down for a couple reasons.' She didn't bother him with details of the others. 'And one of them was to try and see you.'

'I made it onto your personal list,' he chuckled.

'Something like that. You were near the top but don't get a big head about it.'

'Can't wait to see you.' There was a pause during which she held her breath. 'I've been pushing hard down here to get the law suit negotiated to an acceptable solution on both sides so I can spend more time in the Wimmera. You have impeccable timing. I'm bushed for today.'

He was coming back to the country for a

while. Her mood was so light, she teased, 'Just wanted to let you know I'm still a living breathing person here.'

'Oh trust me, I'm well aware of everything about you,' he drawled. 'Can you swing by my office soon and we'll head off somewhere together?'

Addie's heart lifted even higher that he wanted to see her. She always hated making the first move with a guy. 'Sure. I'll head your way now.'

Apart from that fateful interview five years before, Addie hadn't been inside the Chandler building. She remembered it as having a much more casual friendly and inclusive feel than the more formal austere surroundings of Carlton Ross in their renovated heritage building. Where she now realised she had stayed too long in order to advance her career. A decision she had now come to question. Forced by circumstances to leave the company, it was apparent the time was right for a life change. She was feeling so much better for it and positive about her professional future.

Addie took the glass lift to the upper level, the swift ride giving amazing views of Chandler Digital's floor layouts as she sped past each one. Now she was actually here, it was proving hard to imagine Harry in charge of it all. No wonder his life was fully loaded with the responsibility. Yet when he was on the farm with her back home, he seemed perfectly relaxed.

How could he possibly leave all this for a country life? Or manage it from so far away? When the lift stopped and the door slid open, Addie stepped into a wide open space of sofas, floor length windows and a beaming mature receptionist who rose and moved out from behind a nearby glass-topped desk.

'Good afternoon. Ms Kendall?'

'Yes.'

'I'm Emily. Harry's expecting you. He's finishing a meeting but shouldn't be more than five or ten minutes. If you'll follow me.'

Addie was led into a small private space further along still with stunning views and offered tea on a tray already set out on a low table. Emily poured for her, smiled and left.

As Addie sipped, she strolled to the window, admiring the panorama from this end of the city over the skyscrapers of the CBD. When she heard rustling from behind, she turned, smiling, expecting to see Harry. Her delight faded and she caught her breath.

'Adrianna.'

'Mr. Chandler.'

'Austin,' he corrected, striding forward, a gracious older version of his son. With little more than a few distinguished grey hairs since they had last met at her doomed interview, Harry's father hardly seemed to have aged much at all. 'I'm allowed five minutes so this will be brief.'

'Great.' She set down her cup with a clatter and remained standing to face him.

Since meeting Harry again recently, Addie was adapting to but pleasantly challenged by his honesty. It was a positive character trait in his favour but did tend to create confronting moments like these. Which he took upon himself to address and help resolve. She understood his good intentions but the presumption niggled so she waited for Austin to speak.

'Firstly, I appreciate your apparent disappointment some years ago in not gaining employment here.'

No you don't.

Addie withheld her amusement. It was interesting to witness his efforts at an attempted reconciliation of which he would have been completely ignorant if his son hadn't brought it to his attention. Although shocked at the time, she had accepted the decision but allowed it to always irritate her until she opened up to Harry the first day they met again at the creek camp weeks ago. Somehow that admission cleared the mental block and it was no longer an issue. Her solution arrived simply by voicing it.

'In hindsight,' Austin continued, 'I realise I saw you merely as my neighbour Darren Kendall's daughter.'

Of no importance or intelligence because she was a country farm girl? What an attitude. She had never liked this man.

'From that viewpoint,' he droned on, 'I failed to see any future for you with the company despite your academic achievements. This error of judgement became apparent to me within two years of leading the company when my dated management skills weren't in alignment with Harrison's modern progressive style. Despite my experience, I was unsuitable for the top position with Chandler Digital into the future. The reason I stepped aside for my son who has the youth and skills in that regard.'

Yay for Harry.

'This is not an apology-'

Of course not.

'-merely an explanation for my apparently debatable decision in your mind.'

Addie pulled a tight grin but stayed silent, afraid if she opened her mouth she would most certainly put her stylish country boots in it.

Austin grew benevolent. 'My conclusion at the time was to Carlton Ross' gain with fate yet to play its hand.' His mouth almost twitched into a restrained grin.

Addie was fully aware of the irony that she should have been denied employment with the Chandler company only to then be in the place with their opposition five years later to rescue it.

Not appearing entirely comfortable as he did so, Austin looked her directly in the eye with a rather too practised sincerity and said, 'I would like to offer you my deepest thanks for saving

Harrison's company.'

Just words. 'Correct. Harry's company. I did it for him not you.'

That surprised him and he stepped back. 'As you wish. My compliments to your parents when you see them again.'

She made a mental note to pass on the vacant gesture but said nothing.

As quietly as Austin Chandler arrived, he left.

Chapter 13

As though waiting for the surprise meeting to finish between Addie and his father, Harry appeared within moments, grinning.

Confident gorgeous Harry still kicked her pulse up a notch, especially wearing fitted jeans and a casual shirt in the office on a working day over which he now shrugged on a wool-lined leather jacket against the autumn chill outside.

'Hey you.' He pulled her against him for a long slow kiss.

Still recovering from her encounter with Austin and while her whole body hummed with response from the embrace, Addie cautioned, 'Easy on that smile. You set me up.'

Harry shrugged. 'Since he made the suggestion, I thought the old guy deserved an opportunity for his overdue apology.'

'An empty action only made because you told him about my feelings, right? That was a private conversation we had at the creek camp. Geez, Harry. Awkward.'

He pulled away from her. 'I thought-'

'Don't ever think on my behalf. Don't let my size mislead you. Just because I'm ever so slightly shorter than normal doesn't mean I can't handle myself or my problems.' In concession, she added, 'I presume you meant well but it backfired. Your father would never give the slightest thought to a decision he made yesterday let alone five years ago.'

'You've read my father as well as I know him. In my defence, maybe I fell short and didn't have your back years ago but I do now. And always will. Just trying to make amends,' he shrugged, his expression humble.

Addie shook her head and folded her arms. 'Fair enough. Talking so smooth, Chandler, you could be trouble.'

'Troubles are a challenge I like to meet head on.'

'Sounds like a collision course to me.'

'Think of the impact when we connect. All that earth moving under our feet,' he chuckled.

Addie groaned at the corny cliché. 'Don't get ahead of yourself.'

Harry's dark brows dipped into a frown. 'You're annoyed because I set you up with my father. Trust me, I had no hidden agenda. I could see you were bothered by his decision back then and I thought a meeting might help you.'

'It didn't. Because it came from you not him. Honestly, your father is so emotionally dense he clearly gives no second thought that any of his words or actions might affect another human being. And I would certainly never reduce my pride to approach him and point it out.'

'I understand.' She saw the frustration on his face and heard it in his voice. 'Sorry it didn't work out. I apologise.' He sighed. 'I like you and I want to spend time with you. I'm glad you got in touch while you're down. Try to forgive my blunder and don't resist me for too long, okay?' he drawled.

Lost for words, Addie couldn't readily answer. As it turned out, the silence and space between them didn't last because he slipped his hand into hers and entwined their fingers.

'No overthinking, okay?' he murmured.

She nodded. Harry led her back toward the lift. Once inside, reluctantly resigned to overlook his bungled good intentions, she asked, 'So where are we going?'

'Basement carpark.'

She rolled her eyes. 'After that.'

'You'll see.'

As Harry took the bayside roads south away from the city, Addie wondered if he had other pressing matters he should be attending to. 'Are you sure you have time for this?' she carefully voiced her concern.

'I'm sorry you're feeling like an imposition. Sounds like you don't think you're important in my life. My apologies. Again. Obviously I haven't made myself clear enough. I'll work harder on changing that.'

'I don't expect you to change anything for me.'

'I agree. Neither of us should change who we are for the other. But I want to make some life changes and I'd like to think you might be part of that. Perhaps it's the country breaks I've been taking lately and your refreshing company but no matter how busy I've been,' he hinted, 'if I'm honest, maybe deep down I've been more than a little lonely.'

In his demanding corporate and social life? Addie was surprised to hear it but reassured that he trusted her enough to confide such personal feelings.

'I'd like to have a conversation with you about it,' Harry went on, 'but later.' He glanced across at her as he drove. 'Right now let's just enjoy the rest of the day together.'

'Fair enough.'

She could manage that. All the same, the interruption with Austin had thrown her emotions a bit and deep down she wasn't entirely sure why. She was intrigued to know what Harry needed to discuss but determined not to spoil this precious time with him by worrying.

They reached Brighton within thirty minutes yet Addie still had no idea of Harry's ultimate destination. Until they pulled into a foreshore reserve carpark near beachside gardens.

'Up for a walk along the sand?'

'Sure.' She removed her boots and left them in the car.

A soft brisk wind blew in off the bay, coastal

mild, creating rippling onshore waves. They strolled along the shallows for a while, companionably silent, Addie relieved neither of them seemed to feel the need to talk just to fill the air.

She couldn't get her head around Harry taking off half a day to be with her. Quietly slipping his hand into hers, feeling the need to touch and be connected. Buttoning up her denim jacket when they headed out on the long pier. Standing behind, arms wrapped tight and possessive around her when they stopped to watch seagulls almost stationary overhead struggling against the wind, huge tankers and container ships slowly making their way up the bay and into port.

As the afternoon lengthened and the day dwindled, Harry suggested, 'Hungry enough for some dinner soon?'

'I'm not properly dressed.'

'Is that an excuse or a refusal?'

'Neither. Just stating a fact.'

'I'm just wearing jeans. Where do you think we're going?' Addie shook her head and shrugged. 'Leaping to conclusions again. Actually, my favourite restaurants aren't fancy. And relax, we're not eating in. We're eating out. Here.'

He stopped beside the beach kiosk and café, wafting appetizing aromas around passers-by. 'Fish and chips?'

Addie laughed. 'Perfect.'

They carried their white cardboard box of hot and salty battered temptation to the stone wall that separated the pathways and the sand. Sitting on top, licking her fingers and swinging her bare feet, her favourite man by her side, Addie looked across the bay back toward the city, lit up with the dusk. A beautiful sight.

'Best meal in a long while.'

'Agreed. When we can both manage to walk again after such a feast, would you like to come back to my place for a hot drink or a nightcap?'

'You live around here?' Harry nodded. 'I thought the drive here might have a purpose.'

'My four wheel drive could probably find its own way home. I have an electric fire,' he murmured, nudging her knee and shoulders with his own.

'Sounds cosy.'

He slid off the wall, binned their refuse and helped Addie down. Somehow his hands stayed on her waist and he bent for another of his stirring deep kisses.

Addie stood on tiptoe, arms wrapped around his neck. 'You taste yummy and salty.'

'That's a coincidence. So do you.'

Back in his vehicle, Addie put her boots on again for the short drive further along the beach road to his house. As they turned in, private gates slid open and they drove down into a basement garage.

'You have a lift, too?' she said as he pressed a button beside the stairwell door.

'Handy with an armful of groceries.'

'Do you cook?'

'Now that's a loaded question. Do I cook? Yes. *Can* I cook? Debatable. Let's just say when I'm home I manage and occasionally I even risk a roast.'

'Then you're practically a chef.'

While the kettle boiled for her mug of tea and a very fancy automatic coffee machine hummed and bubbled its brew into a pottery cup for Harry, Addie unzipped and kicked off her boots, walking in bare feet again as she trailed around his house, intrigued by what she saw.

Chandler family photos. Random bowls of seashells and pebbles. What looked to be inviting comfortable sofas, the warm tones of oak furniture with a mix of tasteful contemporary and bush landscape artwork on some of the walls. No modern black steel and glass here. The whole ambience felt welcoming and uncluttered, revealing a little more about the person who lived here. Apparently alone.

Knowing Harry better recently, that single situation stunned Addie with disbelief. She backed up against the fake fire until he brought their hot drinks on a tray.

'And chocolates.' She chose a peppermint wrapped in green. 'You can never have too much health food.'

'Love the way your mind works.' Harry settled onto the compact sofa opposite the fire and patted the seat beside him. He sighed and looked around, one arm stretched out behind Addie alongside. 'I'm thinking to move on from here so this may become my beach house.'

She glanced at him in surprise. 'Really? So where's home likely to be next? Somewhere in the Wimmera?' she threw out for fun.

'I could be tempted.'

Addie scoffed. 'Ah yes but you're easily tempted. Take Mum's breakfast for instance.'

'Fair enough but some things take slightly longer to draw me in.'

'Like what?'

'Another person.'

He was staring at her so steadily with those dark absorbing eyes, Harry Chandler took away more than her breath. Surely not. After all these years? Speechless for once, she waited for him to explain.

He didn't waste time on words. Just used very persuasive actions. After which it took a while for them both to resurface to their present setting.

'You really shouldn't have done that. You could spoil a lovely friendship.'

'Friends? Hmm. Is that how you think of me?'

'Not sure. I can't wrap my head around anything more.'

'Please try.' Harry pulled slightly apart, one hand on her knee, the other on her neck with his fingers trailing up into her hair. 'I find you an interesting small package.'

'No need to keep emphasising my lack of height.'

'You make up for it in many other ways.'

'Don't lead me on. A woman might expect more than you're prepared to give and I'm not a plaything.'

'I've known that all our lives.'

'Good. Just so we understand each other.' Addie had locked up her heart against Harry Chandler for safety long ago. But in the light of their recent attraction and mutually warm bond, maybe it was time to find the key and open herself up to possibilities.

To her amusement, he looked decidedly uncomfortable. 'Actually, you scare me.'

'Little me?'

'Yeah. Hard to explain huh?'

Addie grinned and murmured, 'Do your best.'

'She's always been out there but I think I'm finally seeing the real Addie Kendall for myself.'

Without any real warning, apart from the amazing tenderness and sparks of passion they had shared so far, Harry launched right into some emotional territory Addie wasn't so sure she was ready yet to explore with him. Their reconnection had been wonderful but it had only been, like, weeks. Still in the too-good-to-be-true category.

'About our kisses,' he continued, the fire's low flames casting shadows across his face. 'Do anything for you?'

Wow, that question came out of nowhere. 'I get caught up in the moment.'

'Good to know.'

'Where are you heading with this?'

'I've realised recently I've been looking for my kind of woman in the wrong place,' he spoke quietly and slow. 'I'm learning that wherever I am, when we're together, nothing else matters. There's just you and me. And that's enough. I've never experienced that before.'

Okay. Addie needed a moment to take in what Harry had just confided. She heard the words but wondered at his motivations behind them. Hope that there could be something deeper between them? Her heart was certainly keen yet her feelings had been tightly sealed where he was concerned. Being so strong and unreturned so far, Addie remained cautious.

She had this uneasy feeling in the pit of her stomach. Was this for real and actually happening? For starters, they didn't live near each other. A big hurdle. She imagined distance relationships must be challenging. Or was Harry being sentimental after working together recently? She hated to believe it of him when he had protested otherwise but if he was fooling with her…

She pulled away and although not wanting to burst his bubble, said honestly, 'Actually, I don't know too much about the city life Harry, so I'm not sure what you really want or expect of me. This *thing* between us is working at the moment but not everything is meant to last.'

The worldly company CEO, son of a one-time Wimmera grazier who had been educated alongside the Kendalls and other district kids, looked as surprised and unsure after hearing Addie's response, as she was to say it. They weren't teenagers anymore. Heavens, she was pushing awfully close to thirty.

'I hear what you're saying,' Harry said carefully, clearly shaken by what she said, 'but I'd like to give us a shot. Not right this minute or even tomorrow or next week. I can't say too much right now. More information is coming to light on the background to my legal case against Carlton Ross so I have a head full of stuff. Should only be a few more weeks here in Melbourne, a month tops, to see our negotiations through. A lot is happening and new deals need to be made.'

To Addie, it sounded like forever but she couldn't keep her heart boxed up anymore. Maybe it was time to give it wings and freedom. Scary thought, like that first leap of faith over a cliff edge before abseiling down when you couldn't always see the bottom. She had done that a few times with an adventurous boyfriend. Heart stopping yet exhilarating.

So it made sense and she was more than willing to wait for a while until both their lives aligned better. See what the future held for them. If anything. Even if that possibility didn't bear consideration.

'Okay,' she said finally, 'I'll hold you to that.'

'Sounds promising.'

So Harry drove Addie back into the city and took his time over a lingering good night embrace. Alone later in her stripped-bare terrace, she wriggled into a sleeping bag rolled out onto her bedroom mattress.

Jumping into bed with Harry Chandler wasn't out of the question. Addie would be lying to herself if she didn't admit to the odd fantasy of what it would be like between the sheets with him. They were both well and truly consenting adults.

But while their relationship was one of searing attraction, both mutually sensed they still had a journey to travel together. If it worked out, for Addie that would mean a childhood dream coming true. But stepping back, instead of rushing in and forcing a hook-up too early for the sake of it, felt right. For now. Trusting fate and her instinct, she guessed she would know when that moment arrived.

Next day proved equally as busy as yesterday. Although she woke early, having arranged to meet Harry again, there was already a missed call because she always left her phone on silent at night.

Because it could be important news, she redialled the caller. 'Ewan?'

'Addie. Just an update on the homestead find. The skeletal remains found in the cellar have been analysed and classified as a young male. So it can't be Hudson Ross because he was middle aged and there is no DNA match. The Ross family have been informed.'

Addie's first thought was that, in one way, the family would be disappointed. Yet also torn and hopeful that one day they might learn the truth about Hudson. She made a mental note to contact Kimberley to touch base again and at least let her know she was there for her, offer support.

'However,' Ewan continued, 'the remains are a match for an offender on police files. He went missing four months ago. The burglars have talked and provided names, negotiated a deal for their cooperation to be taken into account for a lesser sentence. They have implicated someone so the city team is conducting interviews down there as we speak.'

Addie's head spun at this revelation. The news also meant Holly Duncan at the roadhouse would probably be torn with disappointment at having her own hopes crushed, too, over the disappearance of her mother.

'Thanks for letting me know, Ewan.'

Still sitting on the bed, half out of her

sleeping bag, Addie phoned Kimberley Ross.

'Oh Addie, isn't this just crazy? Everyone assumed and almost wished the body would be Uncle Hudson. I never said anything to father at the time but I didn't see how it could have been. My uncle went missing before the homestead was closed up. My parents only returned to Banyandah after a couple of years. Father forced himself to go through the place, leave some basic furniture and put the rest in storage. You'd think he would have found something then. You know,' Kimberley said, 'he would never admit it but I don't believe my father has ever given up hope.'

'That's blind faith for sure.'

'With the property so isolated and empty, I'm not surprised about burglars and break ins. But someone hiding a body? That's another thing entirely.'

Addie felt sorry the Ross family still had no answer. Wondering how much they knew, she probed, 'Did the police tell you anything about the body?'

'I don't think so. Father would have said when he passed on the information. He was just told it wasn't Uncle Hudson and they were continuing their investigations. Out of courtesy I guess because it involves the homestead.'

'Ewan Holt from back home mentioned it was a young male known to them and missing for a few months.'

'Oh! So the body must have been dumped in the cellar recently?'

'Sounds like it.'

'Thanks for phoning, Addie. You have local contacts and it's so helpful to speak to someone – involved. Quite the coincidence you finding out about our company hacking and now a body in the family homestead.'

'Yeah. Makes you wonder if they're both connected, happening so close together I mean.'

'Who would know,' Kimberley sighed. 'We'll have answers eventually. Life's certainly been complicated lately.'

'Take care. And let me know when we can have that girls' fashion catch-up. I'll come down for the day.'

'Will do.'

Chapter 14

After she hung up, Addie scrambled for the shower ready to meet Harry soon. She had no idea what he might plan for their last few hours together but rummaged through her overnight bag, opting for jeans, a pretty top she had rolled up and tossed in at the last minute, and her favourite denim jacket with her comfortable ankle dress boots.

As she would have expected from a company boss whose daily life was no doubt scheduled down to the last minute, Harry arrived on time. Yet he seemed flexible in allowing time with her when needed.

'Morning.'

They both instinctively leaned in for a long slow kiss.

'I've loaded up Gertie ready to leave later. Do you mind stopping to drop off my house keys to the real estate agent? It's just on Brunswick Street.'

'No problem. It's on our way.'

'To where?'

'You'll find out.'

Turned out they headed for water again. This time to Victoria Harbour marina at the western end of the city. A thriving new development of waterfront living with shops and apartment buildings. They parked and strode along the promenade, stopping before a gleaming and rather comfortable looking sleek white cabin cruiser.

'Yours?' Addie asked, prepared to be impressed.

Harry laughed and shook his head. 'Not my style. Bit of an indulgence. This belongs to a mate.'

He helped her aboard, they settled into their seats and Harry took the controls. At low speed, they edged from their mooring out toward the wide Yarra River.

Harry turned to Addie and grinned. 'Not the Wimmera River or Yarriambiack Creek.'

'Oh, I don't know. Inland waterways have their appeal. Like swinging off a tree rope and dropping from a great height with a decent splash. Baiting up yabby nets and waiting to see what you catch. Can't do that here.'

She cast her gaze to the buildings soaring up either side as they slipped through the calm water. 'In all the years I've lived in the city I've never done this.'

'We often don't really see and appreciate what's literally in our own backyards, no matter where we live.'

'Or maybe the trap these days is that we just don't stop long enough to make the time.'

'True enough.'

Addie thought that quite apart from her career, she would be making even more changes in her life going forward. Thinking of Harry too, the germ of a crazy idea began to take form, depending on how their relationship developed.

Perhaps because both were easier now in each other's company, like their beach stroll late yesterday, they fell silent for a while enjoying the city and river scenery from a new perspective.

They met a rowing eight, and took in the Melbourne Star observation wheel, gazing up in awe as they passed beneath the awesome structure of the Bolte Bridge. Further round, when the river took a sweeping curve, they cruised under the Westgate Freeway. Addie idly noted that she would be taking that route from the city later today.

As the river widened past the container port shipping area with its gigantic loading cranes, the water grew choppy. 'We're escaping to Tasmania, right?'

'Not today. Thought we'd stop at Williamstown. Take a stroll to stretch our sea legs and grab a snack.'

'Great. Haven't been there either,' she said eagerly, having heard from James about the historic bayside village.

'We should be ashamed of ourselves, huh?'

Addie laughed, enjoying the view of a chilled Harry all to herself. Until they separated. Again.

And she returned to the Wimmera. Again.

'What?' Harry caught her staring.

'Just lapping up the company.'

'I'll blush.'

'Big important company guy like you?'

Soon Harry idled back and nudged the boat into its berth to tie up amid a forest of sailing masts at the Williamstown marina. They disembarked and strolled the long pier, hand in hand, a frisky salt-laden breeze gusting in off the water.

A seaplane chugged in from a joy flight as they headed for the main street and shops, crossing a gorgeous central park stunning with burgundy autumn leaves on some grand old trees against the gold of others. They chose one of the many cosy cafes for big mugs of hot chocolate.

As they forked up a shared chocolate dessert, Addie said, 'Probably shouldn't bring up work on your time off but how are the law suit negotiations going with Morgan?'

'My head's full of it anyway.' He reached out for her free hand across the table. 'You're a breathtaking distraction.'

'Stop it,' she whispered, 'or I won't want you to leave later.'

'Now you're talking. Our time will come.'

She sensed it, too, and the promise was exciting.

'With the Carlton Ross case,' he continued, 'I'm not pushing too hard. Don't need to make his life worse right now with all that the family is going through. Initially, their lawyers argued and claimed an error of judgement under difficult financial circumstances. Which is fair enough but no excuse.' He paused and frowned. 'I sensed vibes of something else in the background. And sure enough,' he snapped his fingers, 'the last twenty four hours have brought up alarming new information.'

Harry ran a hand across his face. Addie raised her eyebrows in question and waited. 'My attorneys had already heard a rumour of new developments so we prepared ourselves for that. The reason I've been so damn busy.'

'I didn't mean to-'

'You haven't,' he murmured. 'I needed a break but we're dealing with some astounding stuff.'

When he checked his wristwatch, Addie grinned. 'For a twenty first century guy, you're a puzzle. Most people check the time on their phone.'

'It was a gift from my grandfather,' he explained with a touch of nostalgia. 'Keeps perfect time just like anything digital.'

'Ah. Did you want to leave?'

'I don't want to but we should. It's another hour back to the city. We'll continue this conversation later.'

Addie couldn't wait. She loved that he trusted his confidence would stay between them and wondered what new facts had surfaced in the Ross family and Harry's law suit.

The return trip proved equally relaxing although Addie's appetite was hinting at lunch. She didn't care. Harry would have that covered, too.

From the Docklands marina after mooring the cruiser, Harry drove them south to Albert Park Lake on the city fringe. To a gorgeous restaurant with floor to ceiling windows, a table overlooking the water and uninterrupted views back to the city skyline.

They ordered and chose wines. 'I could get used to this,' Addie admitted.

'But you'd prefer a barbeque in the bush.' Addie shrugged, embarrassed he read her so well. 'Not always my preference either but I wanted to spoil you until we catch up again.'

'You have. It's been a memorable two days.'

When their food arrived and Harry sliced into his steak, he said, 'Remember I mentioned we'd been given further knowledge in the law suit?'

Addie nodded, enjoying her seafood, looking forward to hearing what sounded like yet more revelations.

'Turns out Morgan is covering up for another family member.'

Addie almost choked on her fish and took a long sip of wine. 'It certainly wouldn't be Kimberley so that narrows the field.' Her thoughts raced.

'Try Logan.'

'What! Again?'

'From round table conference discussions, turns out Logan ran up a heap of gambling debts to criminals. To pay it off, he agreed to two things. The first was to give them access on his laptop to the Carlton Ross system so they could hack into Chandler Digital. Apparently he told them we were the biggest competition in the market. They tried to steal information and make money but fortunately failed.

'The second demand was that the crims needed to dispose of a body. They told Logan where it was and to dump it as far away as possible. So he took it into the country one night a few months ago, dumped it in the homestead cellar and padlocked it.'

'Why would he take it so far away?'

Harry shrugged. 'Seems crazy, right? The pressure affected his clear thinking maybe?'

Shocked, Addie gasped, 'So Logan was responsible for the security breach *and* the body?'

Harry nodded. 'When he heard his father discussing their financial situation with the company and that Banyandah needed to go up for sale, apparently Logan panicked and knew he had to get the body out of the cellar. He didn't want to risk returning to the homestead and being seen so he hired the burglars. Once the burglars announced Logan paid them to retrieve the body from the homestead, Logan became a prime suspect for murder until he explained his side of the story to police. They're following up that lead. For his cooperation, he may be fortunate enough to receive a suspended gaol term. Again, the expensive lawyers will go to bat on his behalf and push for a softer sentence, whatever the outcome.'

Addie shook her head in utter disbelief. 'So Logan was just caught up in the consequences of running up gambling debts? I guess he'll think twice before he goes down that path again. You know, that young man always strikes me as being, I don't know, a lost soul maybe? Not knowing what he wants. Still finding his purpose in life. He's probably been carried along by what the Ross family expected of him all his life.'

'A rather grim Morgan assured me his son accepts his mistake and is taking counselling for his gambling habit.' Harry heaved a long sigh. 'So our two companies are seeking a mutually agreeable financial settlement.'

'With Carlton Ross struggling and Logan up for helping criminals, where do they go from here?'

'You know what? We may have it sorted. In a quiet moment while our legal teams were conferring, Morgan looked so bleak. I took him aside and asked him what he wants.'

'And?'

'To sell both the company and the

Banyandah estate homestead and farmland so he can settle with me.'

'Would he even find a buyer willing to take on his ailing company?'

'He may have already found one. My accountants are crunching figures before making an offer.'

Addie's cutlery clattered onto her empty plate. '*You're* thinking of buying Carlton Ross?'

'Possibly. If it's value comes close to reasonable compensation. Knowing all the details now,' Harry admitted, 'I don't want to stick in the boots but I'm also entitled to fair damages.'

'Of course. I see your dilemma. Morgan needing to cash up and redeem his family's legal obligations to settle with you. All because of his son.'

'We might be able to salvage his business model simply by bringing it up to date and combining both companies. That's the head banging stuff my numbers guys are resolving right now.'

Addie held Harry's steady gaze. 'As unfortunate as all this has turned out to be, I'm still proceeding with my unfair dismissal claim.'

'You should. You're entitled. It was what triggered off the whole mess. If you approve,' he offered, 'my lawyers could connect with Jade and bring her up to speed so she has everything she needs to make your case.'

'All right. It would probably save time. I'm

sending you her details now.' Addie tapped them out on her phone.

Harry's mobile pinged and he smiled. 'I'll get them onto it.'

'So,' Addie concluded, 'it's all coming together?'

'Lots of documents and fine print to determine but at least we're heading in the right direction. It's still all going to take a while though.'

Addie understood his gentle warning. She needed to be patient. They dawdled over the last of their meal until she faced the reality of returning home or she would be on the road after dark.

Harry caught her inattention and reflective gazes out over the lake. 'I could kidnap you longer but I guess Gertie's waiting, right?'

Addie scrunched up her nose. 'Yeah. Sorry.'

Reluctantly, they sauntered outside and drove back to retrieve Addie's old car parked outside the terrace, all packed ready to leave.

Lingering, mutually half-hearted about parting, Addie said, 'Thanks for yesterday and today. Now you've explained the depth of discussions and everything involved in your legal case, I appreciate your time even more.'

'Always feel refreshed when I'm with you. I'll get back to the Wimmera as soon as I can.'

'I know. Don't forget me,' she teased, leaning closer.

Harry grabbed her tight and growled, 'Impossible.'

Addie felt in safe and familiar arms when he held, nuzzled and kissed her. Thoroughly. Later, in her rear view mirror, she watched him, hands in pockets, staring back at her as she drove away from the terrace for the last time.

Each time they separated now it was growing harder to tear herself away. A part of her stayed behind and her heart ached. She badly wanted Harry in her life but knew he still had work to do and a life here in the city before they even had the remote possibility of sharing more time together to explore their deepening attraction.

How on earth they would manage that, Addie had no idea and, in order to stay sane, chose not to dwell on the future.

Her family would be shocked by the news she would bring home about the Ross family, Logan's gambling habit that landed him in trouble and the repercussions, his father trying to save him and the family's reputation by getting rid of Addie in the first place. How this had all started.

Not to mention the revelation that the homestead body was not Hudson Ross. So his disappearance, sadly, still remained a mystery, perhaps never to be solved.

Being positive, at least the upheaval of the last few months had brought Harry back into her life but for how long and in what circumstances, she had no idea.

Because she made good time on the highway, Addie stopped by the Coach Roadhouse for Holly Duncan's sake really. The poor girl had been given a teasing sense of false hope for a short time but was no closer to having her own mother's whereabouts resolved.

Addie expressed her regrets across the counter as Holly filled a box of Sid's pastries for her mother. Thoughts of being close to home as she now knew it were more bitter than sweet because it was hundreds of kilometres from the man she loved.

She told herself it wasn't the end of the world. Be patient. As Harry had hinted, their time would come. If that was sooner rather than later, all the better.

Meanwhile, staying positive and concentrating on her new businesses would have to be enough.

Chapter 15

Carl Smith wound down his rental car window, announced himself on the intercom and the security gates to *The Gables* slid open. He slowly cruised along the sweeping drive rising from the exclusive Toorak street. Morgan had done well.

As he pulled up before the mansion and stepped from his vehicle, he admired the formal manicured gardens. Not to his taste. He preferred native bush himself. Having an appointment with Celia Ross he was therefore expected although his identity would remain anonymous until they met. He had claimed to be a generous financial patron. Money always captured Celia's attention.

He was ushered by a uniformed maid through a soaring lobby into a formal sitting room. He did not take the seat offered but remained standing. This meeting would be short.

Within minutes, Celia appeared. At the sight of him, her gracious strides faltered and the polite ready smile vanished.

'Carl Smith?' she sneered bitterly. 'Clever. Carl for your mother Frances Carlton of course and Smith for – obscurity?' She breezed past and turned to face him. 'What can I do for you,

Hudson?'

'Take Banyandah off the market.'

'Why?'

'It's my inheritance. We agreed.'

Celia's thin shoulder shrugged and she said with fake apology, 'Morgan went ahead with having you declared dead.'

'And you didn't correct him.'

'For all I knew, you were.'

'Big mistake. You promised. Do it.'

'You can't want to live in that rotting country pile,' she scoffed.

'That's exactly my plan. I'm back for good. Elizabeth and I will make it our home.'

Celia's thin pencilled eyebrows rose. 'Another woman on the scene at your age?'

'We've known each other longer but married three years ago. I had matters to finalise before we could return.'

She crossed her arms and paced. 'What would Alexandra make of all this?' she taunted.

Celia's slur on his passion for his first wife cut deep. 'Your insults won't work. She would be happy for me. I've made peace with my past. You clearly haven't. You'll always resent me because you embarrassed yourself by making a play for me when everyone knew I was already in love with Alexandra and ignored you when you were, shall I say, *in trouble*. Forcing you to throw yourself at the second son, my unfortunate brother, Morgan.'

'What fantasies. Grief still twists your mind.'

Hudson stepped closer, glaring, and in a smooth calm voice threatened, 'Tell Morgan to remove the homestead from sale or my brother shall know the truth about exactly what happened to the brakes on the vehicle that killed my wife and sons.'

Celia flinched but scoffed, 'I have no idea what you're talking about. A ridiculous accusation, nothing more.'

'Try me. A guilty triple murder verdict will mean life. Either way, my brother will learn the truth and depth of your manipulation to have me *removed* when I was suicidal with depression.'

Celia's gaze narrowed. 'You're bluffing.'

Hudson slowly shook his head and stepped away, half turning. 'Beware Celia. I am fully recovered. Twenty four hours, then I go to Morgan.'

'Where's your proof?' Celia threw at him as he began walking out, clinging desperately to her poise.

Hudson paused but did not turn back. 'In my lawyer's safe, where it has always been,' he said quietly and left.

Celia Ross poured their usual pre-dinner French cognac and handed a crystal tumbler to her husband with a shaky hand, making the ice cube tinkle.

'What's this about?' Morgan scowled.

She took her time before offering a creamy smile. 'Do we really need to sell Banyandah?'

'Absolutely. The extra millions from the homestead and farmland will be vital for us to survive.'

'Being your family heritage property, you wouldn't reconsider? At least for a short time. See how things work out,' she scrambled for words. Losing this persuasion was unthinkable. One of many recently since the Ross empire began to crumble. Morgan was a useless businessman.

'You've never cared for it before,' he challenged.

'I don't particularly,' she tried to sound casual, 'but it will only increase in value.'

'If maintained. It's not. I can't afford to either restore or keep it.' He glanced around the luxurious room. 'It's bad enough hanging onto this money pit. It may need to go, too.'

Celia clutched the exquisite fat double strand of pearls at her neck. '*The Gables*?'

'We can downsize.'

'Never.'

'Not your decision.' Morgan sculled the last of his drink and muttered, 'I have paperwork before dinner. Cleaning up the mess caused by your stupid son.'

'*My* son?'

'You may have thought you trapped me into believing I was the father but I needed your family money, too. We both know Logan's not mine.'

Feeling sick and growing desperate as he walked away, Celia insisted, 'You must reconsider selling the homestead.'

Morgan spun around and, with a loaded suspicious glare, barked, 'Why?'

For that, Celia had no answer. When his wife remained immobile and silent, he disappeared.

Celia Ross sank onto the sofa, legs trembling. With no concession from Morgan, there was no way out. Consumed with misery, she lamented her failure. The number of times she had handed over wads of cash or spread her legs to push the Ross fortunes ahead, could not be all for nothing. How could her life come to this?

Since Morgan refused to sell Banyandah, Hudson's suspicions about the truth surrounding his wife and sons' accident would come out. Straightening her spine, she felt confident she could weather yet another family storm. She had confronted disaster before and prevailed. She always gave a convincing performance when telling lies. She would refute Hudson's claims. His word against hers.

Celia drained her brandy and sighed. At her age, this kind of effort was growing tiresome. Hudson had always been the smart one and, unfortunately, was no fool like his brother. He never did anything without a well-considered reason and planning.

Blast him to hell and back for dismissing her

decades ago in favour of his precious Alexandra. It had been worth a try.

Within days of settling back on the farm, besides her anticipated phone calls and texts from a persistent Harry, Addie received one she was expecting from Kimberley Ross.

Seated before the new desk, overlooking her mother's garden in her freshly redecorated room, she presumed it was in connection with conspiring to launch Stephanie Smythe on a fashion career.

So Addie happily answered. 'Hey, Kimberley.'

'Addie, I have amazing news.'

'Steph has agreed to a meeting?'

'Oh, yes. That, too.' Kimberley's voice faltered, as if she was distracted and Addie sensed something else on her mind. 'But first,' a heartbeat's pause and then she gushed, 'Uncle Hudson is alive.'

Addie's mind blanked and it was a few moments before she could speak. 'He's not! You've seen him?'

Kimberley's composure collapsed and her teary voice wavered, 'We had a family dinner at *The Gables* last night. He's remarried and we met his second wife, Elizabeth. She's just lovely. Oh Addie, he looks so happy. His story is unbelievable. Elizabeth lost her husband and family in an accident, too, and they met at a support group. They're made for each other.'

'Kimberley, I'm blown away. After ten years!'

'I know, right? Best news ever.'

'Your father must be in shock.'

'He is,' Kimberley hesitated then continued, suddenly more strained, her previous joy deflated, 'but it seems mother was involved in my uncle's so called *disappearance*.'

Addie frowned as she listened, wondering how that might have worked at the time.

'Apparently mother persuaded Hudson to disappear. Claimed it was for Hudson's well-being. For the good of the family. Have you ever heard such baloney? Not sure I can ever understand or forgive her for convincing Hudson that was the only way forward out of his grief. I remember how devastated he looked at the funeral. One of the worst days of my life to see him sobbing at the graves of Alexandra and their sons. Just awful, Addie. Not to mention our father's agony over his brother's disappearance and never knowing what happened to him. It's beyond despicable.'

'Yes, the whole thing was such a tragedy for everyone in the district to digest.'

'Horrid for Uncle Hudson at the time but at least he's alive. And looks wonderful. Still the distinguished gentleman as always with a few grey hairs. I'm sure you'll see them in the Wimmera when he and Elizabeth return to

Banyandah.'

'Wow, I guess we will. This is all so much to grasp.'

'Tell me about it. But in the best way.' Kimberley heaved a long shaky sigh. 'Except for mother. You can feel father's anger against her. He's furious over her meddling and deception making him needlessly go through years of grief for his brother. My parents have lived in separate suites for years but this has really blown off the lid. The tension between them is epic. Frankly, I don't see their marriage surviving.'

'Really? Lots of readjustments in the whole family then.'

'Father only had his brother declared legally dead about two years ago. Now that Hudson and Elizabeth intend moving back into Banyandah, father will continue to own and probably sell the surrounding farmland because of course he needs the money. That division of the property was what grandpa Ben intended in his will originally anyway.'

'So it will all work out.'

'The family's getting there but it will still be a long haul.' Kimberley paused and said carefully, 'Have you heard about Logan's involvement in it all?'

Addie hesitated before responding. Best to be honest. 'Harry mentioned. I would never have broken his confidence.'

'It's all right. I know you wouldn't. Just glad

I don't have to explain it all. Mother has always pushed Logan, her favourite child.'

Addie softly moaned, filled with compassion for a daughter pushed aside in favour of her brother.

'It's all right,' Kimberley said, 'I've always known. Now mother can see what her indulgence has done to him. The pressure. She's all about perfection and appearances. She never backs down. Logan has even landed at my apartment just to get away from her and talk. With his future uncertain until all the legalities are finalised, I can only try to be there for him. We're in such turmoil, lots happening and changing but we'll get through it all.' Kimberley took a deep breath and changed the subject. 'Now, about Stephanie. Hope you don't mind but I've rather taken the reins.'

'You know her far better than I do. She just seemed to be a wasted talent. With all that's happening at the moment and your own career, I'm surprised you found the time.'

'You know what? It was a blast calling all my contacts. Kept my mind off family stuff. I was amazed how fast wheels can turn when you set your mind to it. Brilliant suggestion from you by the way, Addie. It has kick started one very happy new fashion designer in a direction she always intended to go. Honestly,' Kimberley sounded so excited, 'you should see Stephanie's portfolio. I feel ashamed but I had no idea how much work she's done. She's already working with a team and in production making her creations. A local boutique clothing manufacturer has made his workshop and highly skilled dressmakers available to her.

'She's aiming for a mid-tier brand range,' Kimberley continued. 'She wants to give her customers value for money and be sharply dressed yet make the body and the budget look good.'

'I'm astounded by all this progress.' Addie almost felt guilty for not contributing more but she had been preoccupied in recent weeks. Besides she lived in the country and Kimberley was on site with connections.

'Once Steph showed her designs she was snapped up and on her way. And producing locally means close control. Tell you what, for a woman who's only been in the industry for five minutes, Steph is on top of everything. She has a wise head on capable shoulders. She's already an utter professional. I'm so proud of her.'

'So with Steph presumably being so busy now is she still seeing Logan?' Addie asked.

'Not as much. She has pulled back but I suspect she still cares for him and wants to see the man emerge from the spoilt boy. She believes in him so at least he'll have some support when he needs it most.'

'If it's meant to happen it will work out between them.'

'True enough. Speaking of relationships, you and Harry?'

Addie often wondered the same thing. 'Going along steadily.'

'You're what he needs, Addie. I've met him a few times at *The Gables* when he's obviously been in meetings with father. It must be a stressful time for him, too, but he looks so much calmer and happier.'

Not knowing the adult Harry well enough before, Addie was unable to compare but touched and hopeful to hear it all the same.

'Now, I hope your calendar is free next month because Stephanie's having her first show of her new design label collection she's calling *Freedom*.' Kimberley named a date, time and venue location on the Yarra River.

Addie laughed. 'My social engagements are thin but even if they were full, I would cancel everything to attend. I'll mark it up in red.'

'Great. There will be an after-party with drinks and nibbles so wear something fabulous.'

Addie groaned with regret. 'I don't usually do fabulous.'

'Then just go as you. I'll see you then.'

Chapter 16

The second Addie hung up, she panicked. What on earth could she wear to do Stephanie proud for the debut fashion show and, creating another opportunity to see him, would Harry be interested to tag along?

The contents of her wardrobe were lamentably inadequate. Mainly crammed with tee shirts, jeans and boots, while a few hangers made a token nod to femininity in the form of pretty maxi dresses.

With Addie's photography website up and running, creating interest and her first orders, she was continually out and about on the motorbike around the farm. Or she jumped in Gertie and explored further afield in the bush closer to the Grampians mountains nearby seeking unique shots to add to her growing collection.

Her first contracts for IT work were trickling in too so her life was becoming busier. And while Harry was in regular touch which fed deeper emotions she hadn't realised she needed, there was also the dilemma of still living with her parents when she had been used to independence. For some reason, she could neither find nor commit to a place of her own. So, while she was reorganising her career options again, the ongoing uncertainty she was feeling left her restless.

With Stephanie's fashion show fast approaching and Harry having readily agreed to accompany her for the night, Addie booked accommodation close to the fashion show venue so she could walk back after it was all over.

She decided to drive down to the city in the morning and give herself plenty of time. So when Addie rumbled up to the boutique hotel entrance in Gertie, the valet's face spread into a beaming smile. While one attendant whisked away her battered overnight case, the other accepted her keys and happily drove the old Holden away for parking.

Preparing for the fashion show toward evening, Addie grew nervous, fussing over her appearance. Totally out of character. All for Harry of course because it was always weeks between seeing each other. Every time they met again, the chemistry was electric. Her pint-sized self wanted to be sexy for him so that if Harry led and took their relationship to the next level, she would be totally on board and ready.

Her mother had assured her you could never go wrong with a little black dress. In Addie's case, ankle length, softly draping her figure and at least giving the illusion she was taller, with killer heels on her dressy shoes adding definite vital inches.

Back at the farm, her mother had produced a

special piece of family heirloom jewellery. A delicate filigree vintage chandelier necklace of amethyst teardrops and gold Julie wore for her wedding to Addie's father, handed down from her own mother and grandmother. Now it sat perfectly around her neck and glittered against the dark dress.

Never inclined to impress, tonight Addie had arranged to meet Harry in the hotel lobby so she could take her time walking up to him and savour the thrilling vision. She only hoped she wasn't under-dressed. He was such a heartthrob, she simply wanted to complement him.

Her mobile pinged. He was here.

As Addie stepped from the lift, they simultaneously caught sight of each other because he was watching for her arrival. Classy looking jeans with a white collarless shirt, a little flick to informality, topped off by a silky black jacket all of which were perfectly fitted to every inch of his gorgeous body. Addie grew hot and her heart raced at the sight.

Harry grabbed her hand and tugged her close to whisper, 'I missed you.' He pressed warm lips to her cheek. 'Don't want to ruin your lipstick. Yet,' he drawled. As they left the hotel, he added, 'By the way, you're gorgeous.'

'Thank you.'

Harry drew her arm through his and they strolled along the waterfront the short distance to Stephanie's fashion show. The venue delivered.

Exposed brick walls and beams, candles, flowers, all combined to present simple and classic understated elegance. A low runway ran down the centre of the room. Fashionable and influential people mingled, sipping wine, crowding the room that buzzed with chatter.

The guest of honour, clearly busy backstage, was nowhere to be seen. Logan Ross, however, quietly hovered behind his mother, Celia, as the guests all began taking their seats.

Further along, Addie noticed Kimberley seated in a front row next to her father, perhaps supporting his daughter. Her friend smiled and waved. It was the first time Addie had seen Morgan since the day of her formal termination in his office. He caught her eye but she ignored him, still unable to excuse her dismissal to protect his weak son. Since they all sat apart, it was obvious the Ross family had splintered into factions.

James blew her a kiss as he arrived with Michael, both trendy in pastel suits and, although she couldn't see his feet, probably his Nota shoes!

A pleasant surprise for the evening was a familiar face Addie hadn't seen in years. Harry's mother, accompanied by a female friend. They approached and paused before them.

Harry rose and kissed her cheek. 'Mother, you remember Addie Kendall?'

'I certainly do. Lovely to see you, my dear.'

'Mrs. Chandler,' Addie smiled.

'Isabelle,' she said warmly, her grey hair elegantly upswept, wearing a simple dress and sensible low heeled, if glitzy shoes. 'And this is my good friend and neighbour, Adele.'

Then the lights dimmed, Kimberley rose from her seat and, at the end of the stage, took the microphone to welcome everyone to the launch of up and coming designer, Stephanie Smythe's, first *Freedom* collection.

One by one, classic feminine and dreamy gowns emerged from behind curtains at the far end. And, best of all, there wasn't a gaunt model in sight. Inspiring to see fashions worn by real women. Some tall and, to Addie's delight, some short. Clearly chosen for their suitability to showcase each gown to its best advantage.

Stephanie's appearance at the end drew resounding applause then guests and models, still in their gowns and circulating, all moved into an adjoining room with long tables of food and drink. Harry found them glasses of champagne.

As soon as a popular Stephanie was free, Addie congratulated her with a smile and a hug on the undeniable success of the evening.

'I understand you had a hand in all this,' Stephanie beamed. 'Thank you for the push I needed. And can you believe all the contacts Kim has produced to support me?'

Logan quietly appeared by her side.

Feeling a combination of repulsion and pity, Addie kept it casual. 'Hey, Logan. It's been a while.'

He offered nothing more than a desultory response and a faint smile. The playboy still lurked underneath but there was a guarded edge to him now that Addie certainly didn't remember from childhood. Being the star of the evening and in demand, Stephanie was soon drawn aside by other guests.

When Kimberley advanced on Addie, thankfully alone without her father, Harry made his excuses and drifted away toward his mother.

'Don't worry,' Kimberley assured her. 'I waited until father was distracted. I didn't expect you would care to speak to him.'

'No.'

'He's ploughing all his energy into his old passion and new career in art investment. He's been an interested collector all his life, his acquisitions all stored in the basement at *The Gables*. Father studied art history at university, the story of humanity by examining the past.'

Addie wondered if all Kimberley's talk of her father moving on was meant to portray him in a new and favourable light. Frankly, she didn't care if he had a lemonade stand on a local beach or spoke at the United Nations. In her mind, the damage to his credibility and nepotism at her expense had been done. She could care less.

'His interest covers all the artistic periods and movements including our own Aboriginal culture and indigenous artists.'

Disinterested in anything to do with Morgan Ross, Addie had zoned out but concentrated again with Kimberley's statement. 'Is aboriginal art an investment?'

'Absolutely. Original works can claim huge prices and not only retain their value, but often dramatically increase. A wise investment for sure.'

'Good to know.' Addie filed that information away for future reference in case she came across any Piper Thorne artwork.

Her gaze roamed the room to settle on Harry and, of all people, Morgan Ross standing together in what looked like polite conversation.

Kimberley saw the direction of her steady glance. 'Young Chandler is looking magnificent tonight.'

Addie grinned. She found herself scrambling for words to respond when anyone teased or even casually mentioned her friendship with Harry. After years of secretly holding an attraction for the man, their present magnetism seemed incredible and fragile. For the most part this evening, Harry hadn't moved far from Addie's side. Whenever she looked, he was always there and she felt crazily pleased by his devotion.

All night when they shared a glance and smile, the significance behind Harry's gaze held a new and deeper meaning.

After Kimberley moved on, Harry was back by Addie's side with fresh drinks and a plate of nibbles to share. She had noticed her lawyer, Jade, among the guests and the stunning woman now wove her way through the crowd toward them.

After greetings, Jade said, 'Just a quick word, Addie. Carlton Ross have made an offer. Drop into the office in the morning before you leave.'

'Sure.' Maybe she could finally ditch the phantom of Carlton Ross from her life if their pitch impressed enough to look like a fitting settlement and apology.

As the evening grew late and the fashion crowd gradually thinned, Harry murmured, 'Just say the word and I can walk you back to your hotel.'

Addie nodded, grateful to escape. She liked Kimberley and Stephanie and wished the latter every success for *Freedom* but this world was not her scene. The more time she spent back home in the Wimmera, even though it meant being parted from Harry, the more she was certain that was the life she wanted and where she was meant to be.

As she and Harry strolled, the lights along the riverbank reflected in the water.

In the hotel lobby, still holding hands, Addie suggested, 'Want to explore the mini bar in my room?'

'Now that's an offer I wouldn't refuse.'

In her suite, the open drapes provided a stream of city glow and moonlight that bathed the room. Addie kicked off her shoes, Harry wandered over to the minibar fridge for two beers and joined her on the sofa.

Seated close together and with the charged atmosphere in the shadowy room, Addie's body stirred when Harry slid an arm about her shoulder. She snuggled against him. Her favourite place in the world as they sipped beer and let the gentle night flow around them.

Her own personal country bloke, dark hair falling softly across his forehead. Addie didn't resist combing her fingers through to brush it back. Harry's eyes lit with an exciting dangerous light, making deep joy bloom inside her as his finger traced the curve of her mouth.

'You're getting to me, Addie Kendall. I'm finding you sexy and you're not even trying.' His voice was rough with emotion. 'I think I've finally found where I belong.'

Breathless, she clung tight, their heartbeats pounding together. 'And where would that be?' she managed to say.

'With you. If you're interested,' he said hopefully.

Addie moaned against Harry's shirt and spread her hands out across his chest. Confused. Amazed. 'You can't do this to me, Chandler. Not after twenty years of waiting since I was five years old and started school and there you were. Already a handsome mystery.' She tilted her head back to look at him. 'Don't mess with me, Harry.'

He kissed her. 'I'm not.'

'This thing inside me that I feel for you is big.'

He kissed her again. 'I know. It's real for me, too. I'm in.'

That was it? 'I'm a country person,' she pointed out.

'I will be too.'

She hoped her raised eyebrows and stunned gaze told him she needed a bit more information than that. 'Really? When is this happening?'

'Soon as I finish up down here. I have plans.'

With slow purpose, Harry began blazing kisses over any bare skin he could find on the woman in his arms. The dip of her neck, her cheeks, her lips. Addie chuckled with delight but their beers were getting in the way so they set them aside.

Reuniting again, Harry's hands cupped her face. 'I promise one day soon we won't have to leave each other.'

Addie's heart filled with love. Feeling shameless, she suggested, 'I don't suppose we could start that habit, like, tonight?'

Harry's eyes flashed with passion and he treated her to a lazy grin. 'I don't see why not.'

'You don't feel like you're being taken advantage of by a rather wicked country girl?'

'They're the best kind.'

His mouth covered hers, effectively stopping any further conversation. Addie sighed. About time. She was tired of talking.

And then it all happened with such ease and familiarity, as natural as breathing.

Harry unbound her long blonde hair, letting it down and loose, looking riotously windblown as though she had ridden her motorbike without a helmet. They took their time. Slow was good. Removing one piece of clothing from each other in turn. She felt Harry's fingers gliding down her back unzipping her dress.

Until they had wriggled free of almost everything except the necklace. When Addie raised her arms to unfasten it, Harry stalled her with his hands, scooped her into his arms and they tumbled onto the bed. Then they wound themselves around each other amid wild kisses to embark on creating an unforgettable memory.

Next morning, Addie woke to daylight streaming into the hotel suite. To the smell of coffee and bacon and the sight of a loaded breakfast trolley. And Harry, clad only in his shorts and a shirt left hanging open, revealing the toned bare chest that had pressed against hers last night.

Half sitting up in bed, leaning on her elbows, she sighed over the vision and the recollection of opening her heart to unimaginable bliss on the most exciting night of her life. So far. She looked forward to many more.

'If that sheet falls any lower, I'll have to come over and ravish you again,' he growled.

Addie smiled, pulled on a hotel robe and joined him at the table but not before stealing a long lush kiss.

'Morning,' she whispered.

'I love you.'

Addie's heart tumbled over at the depth of love on his face and reflected in his eyes. 'That's nice.'

Impossible to hide the special glow of falling in love. But until they both resolved their lives enough to be together, there would still be days like this when they would part to go their separate ways.

Addie couldn't imagine her life without Harry Chandler in it now so leave-taking later was emotional agony. The next time they met, he better make the drought worthwhile.

Chapter 17

Three weeks later

No one living and farming the dry Wimmera plains ever complained about rain. With loads of the watery stuff having fallen over recent weeks, the seasonal break looked promising. It created mini lakes in paddocks, temporary swamps, and set creeks and rivers running.

The crops Addie's father and brothers had worked around the clock sowing had sprouted and the Wimmera was tinged in lush green. As always, throughout the busy cropping season, her mother had kept everyone well fed.

With the pressure eased, the Kendall family social life sprang into a welcome return. Most importantly, a celebration for the successful resolution of both Harry's IT law suit and buy-out of Carlton Ross, and Addie's unfair dismissal claim.

The company's acceptance of her compensation claim came with a formal legal letter of apology and a reference detailing her employment criteria during her contract with the company. Filled with relief when she read it, Addie considered the reparation officially closed the matter of the recent unfortunate chapter in her life. For which she couldn't be entirely ungrateful. It had brought Harry back into her life.

The porch screen door whined as Addie pushed it open with her backside, one hand balancing a salad platter, the other a basket of freshly sliced crusty breads. Out on the patio, smaller tables were pushed together to create one long food feast with chairs all around.

The family dogs, Rowdy and Bandit, nosed around underfoot, lapping up any spare attention.

Addie joined her mother, sorting cutlery and paper napkins. 'New neighbours haven't arrived yet.'

'Beth said they might be late. Apparently Hudson's up ladders painting. She didn't sound impressed,' Julie chuckled. 'I imagine it's a labour of love and a matter of personal pride for him to put work back into restoring the family homestead.'

Darren was wrapped in his usual full length grilling apron in charge of all things barbeque. The laundry trough was filled with ice and drinks. All morning in the kitchen, Julie, Addie and Jen Campbell had prepared salads and vegetables.

Addie wouldn't be surprised if Jen and Lachie were partners now. Judging by the looks and touches between them these days, she recognised the feeling. One farmer down maybe, two to go?

Nick, her larrikin charmer brother, was a magnet for local girls but one of them would steal his heart when he least expected it. At some point, Mitch, the youngest, the quiet one, would suddenly surprise them all by bringing home the girl who shared his love of farm life and the country.

With winter officially on the horizon, everyone was rugged up in warm clothes, thick checked winter shirts, windcheaters, hoodies and jeans. No fancy clothes out here.

A variety of mud-splattered cars parked everywhere in the gravelled yard. A familiar four wheel drive pulled up to join them. With all the family here, its owner was the first guest to arrive.

'Chandler's keen,' one of her brothers teased.

Addie ignored him and strode out to greet her man, rewarded with his heart-stopping smile and kiss. Harry phoned every night so the family all recognised an obvious change in their relationship. Her parents knew she was a big girl now, intelligent and independent. They tactfully watched and smiled and didn't ask questions.

Not long after Harry appeared, the Kendall's latest nearby residents arrived.

Addie recognised and remembered Hudson Ross the first time they met again recently. Still the same deceptively unassuming man, slightly older and greyer, who had held her at arm's length, obviously updating his memory before she was warmly hugged in greeting.

The heartfelt gesture charmed her, revealing perhaps an understandable measure of regret for a life reluctantly placed on hold. Bringing home to Addie the yawning difference between the two Ross brothers, Hudson and Morgan.

Addie totally agreed with Kimberley's initial assessment of her new aunt Elizabeth. Beth Ross *was* lovely and natural with a ready smile and impulsive laugh. The controversial district couple had already quietly slid into the local community. The Ross and Kendall families had now become regular visitors in each other's homes.

Beth made light of their renovation circumstances. 'It's like camping but it won't be forever.'

She and Hudson were well underway with what they called their *retirement project* to completely restore the homestead and re-landscape the gardens. With the full intention to hold garden parties and open house days in the historic residence to raise money for local fundraising causes. All with the aim of dispelling the stigma of its recent past and making Banyandah a warm and welcoming home again.

With plates and glasses filled, the chilly outdoor air filled with conversation and laughter, the celebratory barbeque lunch kicked on into the afternoon.

Harry took Addie aside. 'Something I'd like to show you before dark.'

One of her brothers obviously overheard and yet again teased, 'Keep it decent, Chandler. That's our little sister.'

Addie closed her eyes and shook her head. Really? Harry usually took the ribbing in his stride but when she opened them again, she noticed that her big strong city bloke was blushing and embarrassed. They shared a private glance, only the two of them knowing how indecent their little sister had actually been with this man.

She took his cue and willingly accepted the chance to escape and steal some private time with Harry.

'Is this another mystery tour like the drive to your Brighton house and our boat trip out to Williamstown?' They had driven district roads for fifteen minutes.

'Actually, we've arrived.' Harry stopped on a gravelled verge opposite paddocks dotted with big old gum trees like a bush parkland that stretched away forever.

But when Addie turned, they had a clear distant view of the purple blue Grampians mountains. 'There's nothing here.'

'Don't be impatient. These things take time.'

Harry helped Addie through the wire fence. As they strolled across, he said, 'This land's for sale. It would make a great site for a family home. What do you reckon?'

Addie grew ridiculously excited when she tweaked to his purpose. 'That's why you brought me here? A romantic bush setting. It was a trap, right? Get her to like the place and she'll like me.'

'Oh, I think we're both in over our heads a bit deeper than that,' he drawled. 'I'm thinking something rustic, passive solar. Only a few clicks into town.'

'So you're suggesting we set up house together?'

'More or less,' he shrugged.

'You've lived in the city a long time,' Addie reminded him.

'Used to,' he corrected. 'I'm making a tree change, remember? Permanently.'

'What about your company?'

'All details for distance management are securely in the pipeline.'

His mouth curled up a little at the edges and his gaze was so honest she almost broke down and cried with crazy happy disbelief. 'Are you going to keep that kiss on your lips all to yourself or share it with me?'

He didn't have time to finish because Addie stood on tiptoe to reach him, slid her arms around his neck and pulled him down for a kiss she intended he would never forget.

'I love you, Addie Kendall.'

'I know. Ditto. You've had my heart a long time,' she whispered. 'I've always loved you, even when you weren't around. So it's a no-brainer for us really, isn't it?'

'Any idea what you want our future to look like? Living together? Waiting? We can be partners or I can propose. Tell me how you want us to be.'

'Your folks and mine are life timers. I like the look of that.'

'Thought you would.' He moved her slightly away from him to reach into the pocket of his jeans. There was no tiny velvet box and he didn't get down on one knee. He simply held up a ring between a thumb and forefinger. As clouds parted, it twinkled in the pale early evening sunlight.

'When our grandmother died, since she only had grandsons, she let Oliver and I each choose one heirloom piece of jewellery.' He dangled it in front of her. 'I've been waiting a long time to give this to the right person. Adrianna Kendall, will you marry me sometime and make us both happy?'

'Cripes, Chandler, you sure know how to knock a simple country girl sideways off her boots. But I have to say, I'm getting to like surprises. Answer's yes. On two conditions.'

'What?'

'You don't wait another twenty years to put that ring on my finger.'

Harry watched her face the whole time he slowly did just that. Then, backed up against the rough ridges of the tree bark, they kissed again, and again.

'And what's the second?'

'Let's see how we progress, huh? I know marriage is the traditional way but to last a lifetime it not only takes a backbone of love but also respect, perseverance and a ton of communication. I've watched my own parents' tolerance and acceptance of each other and I've seen other marriages fold after a few years. We both have businesses to run and a working life to consider but I'd love to spend time travelling the world with you. See how we go on together.'

Harry's dark eyebrows rose in surprise but he was smiling. 'Sounds like a plan. I just want you to be happy and for us to be together.'

The cooling late autumn breeze rustled through the dry eucalypt branches high overhead as they kissed again.

Addie adored this man, always had and sensed she probably always would. They had some ground to cover before this relationship evolved enough to see whether their lives and personalities were a long term fit. She had learned to trust her usually reliable instinct but always kept an open mind and heart.

Where Harry was concerned, the future was looking good and she had a feeling, when the time was right, they wouldn't have far to go to a certain neighbouring homestead to celebrate that bush garden wedding she had always dreamed about. And a fashion designer friend who would make *the dress*.

There would be highs and lows but they held a trump card, a deep and genuine love. With communication, respect and laughter, like the unpredictable Wimmera seasons, she hoped over time they would weather them and endure.

As they tramped back toward Harry's vehicle over twigs and dry leaves and the occasional field mushroom, he said, 'So we're winging it, then?'

'Pretty much. We have a lot to learn about each other. We'll work it out.'

'Want kids?'

She glanced sideways and grinned. 'Absolutely. Eventually,' she cautioned.

'How many?'

Addie laughed. 'Whatever comes along. Harry Chandler. Don't be impatient,' she mimicked. 'These things take time.'

www.ingramcontent.com/pod-product-compliance
Lightning Source LLC
Chambersburg PA
CBHW061031120726
47910CB00006B/2194